Never Be The Same

A Novel By

Silk White

Good2Go Publishing

Published by:
GOOD2GO PUBLISHING
7311 W. Glass Lane
Laveen, AZ 85339
www.good2gopublishing.com
www.silkwhite.com
facebook/silkwhite
twitter @good2gobooks
silkwhite212@yahoo.com
G2G@good2gopublishing.com
Facebook.com/good2gopublishing
ThirdLane Marketing: Brian James
Brian@good2gopublishing.com

Cover design: Davida Baldwin
Edited by: M.S.Hunter
Typesetter: Rukyyah
ISBN: 978-0-615-63017-5

Acknowledgement

Thanks to all of my fans for riding with me...
Enjoy!

The Start of It All

Paige stood in front of a full length mirror applying lotion on her naked body something she did when she got out of the shower. Paige was excited because today was the day her man Jeezy was returning home from a weekend trip out of town. Just the thought of her man coming home brought a smile to Paige's face. The two had been together for six years and were madly in love with each other. Paige threw on a pair of her black Good2go leggings and a wife beater as she headed downstairs. Two years prior Jeezy had surprised her with a new 3,996 square foot house. When Paige made her way downstairs she saw that the kitchen table was covered with money. "Shit!" she cursed. How could she forget that Jeezy had asked her to count and rubber band the money up for him before he came back? Paige quickly sat down at the table and began counting up the loose bills, making 5k stacks. Paige was a professional actor and loved what she did for a living, but whenever Jeezy needed her to do anything for him she would always hold him down. Jeezy had made sure Paige was well taken care of since she was the one who gave him money to start his empire. It was the money she had made from her first acting gig that helped Jeezy become the man he was today. Paige sat at the table placing rubber bands on the money when the front door busted open. BOOM!

"F.B.I" A man yelled with his gun aimed at Paige's head. She stood in shock as she watched what looked like one hundred special agents bum rush her home with each man wearing riot gear.

"Down on the floor!" Another agent yelled. Before Paige even got a chance to comply another agent viciously clothes lined her out of her seat and on to the floor where they hand cuffed her.

"What the fuck are y'all doing?" Paige yelled from the floor as she watched the federal agents ransack her home looking for any kind of contraband. Paige knew Jeezy never kept any product in their home so she wasn't worried about them finding anything. What she was worried about was all of the tax free money that rested on the kitchen table.

"I want to see the warrant!" Paige yelled. She knew how dirty the police could be at times. She wanted to make sure they had the right to be all up in her house searching through her personal belongings.

"Bitch you don't speak unless you're spoken to!" A white man wearing a suit growled. The white man's name was Andy Smith and he was the lead F.B.I agent on the case. He and Jeezy had history. Andy had pinned three cases on Jeezy, but somehow he and his big shot lawyer always seemed to beat all the charges every time; but this time was going to be different. Andy walked upstairs and ten minutes later he returned carrying a Ziploc bag full of cocaine.

"What have we here?" Andy smiled as he stood in front of Paige dangling the Ziploc bag in her face.

"That shit ain't mine and you know it!" Paige spat.

"Well I found it here in your home" Andy said sarcastically. "Now listen to me and you listen to me carefully you little bitch" he said letting the words slide off his tongue. "I know these drugs belong to your little petty hustling boyfriend Jeezy" he told her. "All you have to do is testify that the drugs are his and you are free to go."

"Fuck you!" Paige said looking at Andy like he was insane. Andy shook his head. "So you're willing to give up everything for this scum bag?" he asked. "What about your acting career? I saw those three movies you were in and I know the next movie roll you get is going to be paying in the millions. Are you really willing to give all that up for a lowlife hoodlum that wouldn't do the same for you?"

Tears slid down Paige's face as she opened her mouth to speak. "I need to speak to my lawyer."

"You dumb cunt!" Andy growled as he turned and punched Paige in the stomach. He watched as she dropped down to her knees and began coughing. "Get this trash out of my site" he said with a wave of his hand. Paige cried as she heard the other agents destroy her house as they escorted her outside. Paige walked out the house with her head down as she passed by all the other agents and news crews that had arrived on the scene hoping to get a juicy story. All that was going through Paige's mind was where the hell was Jeezy?

***

Jeezy pulled up a block away from his crib in his 600 Benz and looked on in shock. He couldn't believe what his eyes were seeing. He saw flashing lights everywhere as F.B.I agents walked on his property like it was theirs. As Jeezy sat back watching he wondered what the F.B.I was doing at his house. Ever since his last case he'd started hustling out of town in an attempt to keep stick up kids and cops away from his home. He watched as two agents brought Paige out of the house in handcuffs. She had a scared looked on her face as the agents roughly shoved her in the back seat of one of their squad cars.

Jeezy quickly threw his Benz in reverse and backed up to the next street. He didn't know what was going on but one thing he knew was that Paige was going to need a lawyer.

On the way to his lawyer's office, a million thoughts ran through his mind. The first thing Jeezy thought about was did someone snitch on him and if so who? Why else would the FEDS just run up in his crib?

Jeezy stormed inside his lawyer's office and helped himself to a seat. "The fucking FEDS just kicked my door down and arrested my fiancé" he huffed.

"Slow down" Mr. Goldberg said as he leaned back in his expensive looking chair. "Now start from the beginning."

"I pulled up to my crib and saw the FEDS everywhere" Jeezy said in a fast tone. "They took my girl. I need you to represent her and find out what the charges are."

"I got you" Mr. Goldberg said. "But more than likely they were there for you so what I need you to do is to lay low until I find out exactly what's going on."

"When will you have some answers for me?"

"No later than tomorrow morning" Mr. Goldberg assured him. "I'll get on it right now."

"I appreciate it" Jeezy said as he stood and shook his lawyer's hand. He then made his exit.

Jeezy pulled up in front of The London hotel and let the valet attendant park his Benz. After everything that had gone down at his home, there was no way Jeezy could go back there tonight. Instead he settled for the nice five star hotel downtown. When Jeezy stepped in his room he quickly checked the entire room making sure he was alone. This was a habit he had picked up from dealing in the underworld. Once the coast was clear he removed his 40 caliber from his waist, tossed it on the bed, and headed straight for the shower. In the shower Jeezy aimed the shower head directly on his face as he thought about the seriousness that Paige could be facing ahead because of him. There was no way Jeezy could let his fiancé do jail time because of his dealings in the streets. He promised himself that he would never go back to jail, but now he was in a difficult situation. If Paige went to jail she would lose everything that she had worked so hard for. All the acting classes and the endless nights of her being up all night trying to memorize her lines would all be for nothing. Being a man, Jeezy couldn't let Paige go out like that. So while in the shower Jeezy mentally prepared himself to take the charge and do the time so Paige would be free.

Jeezy hopped out the shower and turned the TV to SportsCenter as he lay wildly across the bed until he fell sound asleep.

Ride or Die

The next day Jeezy sat leaning on the hood of his Benz in front of the courthouse. Paige's bail was $20,000. The price hurt Jeezy's pockets but he had to get his woman out of jail. Twenty minutes later Paige exited the courthouse with Mr. Goldberg by her side. As soon as she spotted Jeezy she smiled. Everyone called him Jeezy because he favored the famous rapper Young Jeezy.

"Hey baby" Paige sang as she slid in her man's arms. "It feels so fucking good to be up out of that piece of shit!"

Jeezy smiled as he stroked Paige's hair gently. "You ain't got to worry about ever going back up in there ever again."

"It's no way I'm going to be able to beat this case baby and you know it" Paige said. "Even Mr. Goldberg said it would be best to take a deal."

"Fuck a deal" Jeezy said. "I'm not just gonna sit back and let my woman go to jail. I'll take the charge baby. It was me they were looking for anyway."

"Not so fast" Mr. Goldberg cut in. He knew Jeezy was trying to get his girl off the hook, but getting her off the hook didn't seem like the best move at the time to him. "You might want to re-think that idea. With your record they can easily give you fifteen years." "You'll probably get out in twelve. Now her on the other hand" Mr. Goldberg said looking over at

SILK WHITE

Paige. "If you eat this charge the most time you can get is five years tops and you'll be out in three since you have a squeaky clean record. I'm not telling yall what to do, but yall might want to go home and talk about this a little more."

"What home" Paige chuckled. "They put a freeze on all of our shit until they see what happens with the case. We can't go back there. That house belongs to the FEDS now."
Jeezy stood on the sideline and just shook his head. All the hard work that he and Paige had put in over the years was all spinning down the drain right in front of his eyes. Everything they had worked for the FEDS were about to take, including their freedom.

"Come on baby let's get up outta here" Jeezy said holding the passenger side door open for Paige to get in. "I'll give you a call tomorrow" he said as he shook Mr. Goldberg's hand and walked around the Benz. He hopped in the front seat. For the entire ride back to the hotel Jeezy listened to Paige complain about how nasty and filthy the jail was. The sad thing about it was she had only been there for one night so in his mind Jeezy knew it was no way she would be able to do five years in a place like that. Jail wasn't for certain people and Paige was one of those people. She wasn't cut out to be in jail and Jeezy knew it. When the two made it inside their home Paige took a quick shower. She hopped out dried off and laid across the bed. "What you over there thinking about" she asked looking over at Jeezy.

"Thinking about this twelve years I got in front of me" Jeezy sighed. Jail was the last place he wanted to be especially for over a century, but he knew he had to do what he had to do.

Paige laughed and said "Baby come sit down over here." She patted a spot on the bed next to her. "If you think I'm letting my man go to jail for twelve years you must be crazy."

"But baby..."

Paige raised her hand quickly hushing him. "Three years is better than twelve years anyway you put it. I know you trying to look out for me, but this time I have to look out for you."

Jeezy wanted to protest, but he knew what she was saying was right. He knew Paige would do the time for him. The problem was he didn't want his girl stuck in a place like that for three long years.

"It won't be too bad." Paige smiled on the outside, but on the inside she felt like shit. She valued her freedom, but she loved her man and would do anything for him. "I'm a big girl. You just hold it down while I'm in there."

"You sure you don't want to think about this a little longer before you make this decision" Jeezy asked?

Paige replied by kissing Jeezy on his lips. She then worked her way downtown until she reached his manhood. Jeezy moaned as Paige took him all the way in her mouth like an expert. Jeezy looked down and watched as Paige sucked the shit out of his dick. She moaned loudly as she sloppily sucked and jerked his dick at the same time until Jeezy forced her to stop. He aggressively flipped her over on her stomach as he entered her from behind. Paige moaned loudly as Jeezy filled her insides. Jeezy fucked Paige as if he was punishing her. He tore her pussy up until he couldn't take it no more and exploded.

For the rest of the night Jeezy and Paige sat up getting drunk, discussing their future plans, and mapping everything out until they fell asleep in each other's arms.

Lock In

Jeezy pulled the Benz up a block away from the courthouse and cut the engine off. Today was the big day. Paige was looking nervous and scared to death. She didn't want to go to jail for three years, but she had to do what she had to do.

"You alright" Jeezy asked as the two hopped out of the car and headed towards the front of the courthouse.

"No, everything is not alright" Paige said turning to face Jeezy. "I need you to make me a few promises before I go and do this time for you."

"What's up" Jeezy said giving Paige his full attention.

"Don't speak I just need you to listen" Paige said as tears rolled down her face. "I'm about to be gone for three years and I know a man is going to be a man. Just please promise me that whatever bitch you start dealing with while I'm gone…"

"What are you talking about" Jeezy interrupted with a confused look on his face.

"Whatever chick or chicks you start dealing with while I'm gone please let them know their place and you better let them know that your queen will be home in three years. Promise me that you won't get anybody pregnant or fall in love with another woman and forget about me while I'm gone and you better marry me when I get out."

"Never baby" Jeezy said pulling Paige in close for a hug. He knew all kind of crazy thoughts were running through her mind right now and the fear of the unexpected awaited her. "It's me and you against the world. Fuck everybody else. The last thing on my mind is a bitch" he told her. "My focus is on rebuilding the empire and having everything set up by the time you get out and yes we will get married as soon as you get out."

"I love you so much baby" Paige cried. "I miss you already."

"I know baby. I know." Jeezy said as the two hugged in front of the court house.

Paige sighed loudly as she wiped away her tears. "Let's go get this shit over with." The two stepped in the courthouse and were met by Mr. Goldberg.

Jeezy sat in the back of the courtroom and watched as the judge sentenced his fiancé to three years. Paige looked back at Jeezy as the officers escorted her to the back and mouthed the words "I love you." Jeezy watched as Paige disappeared into the back. At that very moment he felt like his soul had just been ripped out of his body.

"Those three years are going to fly by in no time" Mr. Goldberg said as he patted Jeezy on the back. "She's going to a federal correctional facility. I'm not sure which one yet, but I'll have that info for you by the end of the day."

"Thanks and I appreciate it" Jeezy said as he hurried out of the courtroom. Now that Paige was gone his main focus was getting money. Ever since the raid on his home, the lawyer fees, and Paige's bail money Jeezy's stash was on E. He hopped in his Benz and headed straight to Montana's house.

Montana was Jeezy's connect. He was originally from Miami. Montana moved to New York and started his drug business. Montana and Jeezy had been doing business together for the past three years. Montana was a good guy, but he was about his money and didn't take any shit from anybody. Whenever he sensed a problem he would quickly eliminate it.

Jeezy pulled up in front of Montana's house and quickly hopped out the car heading for the front door. He rang the doorbell and patiently waited. Finally one of Montana's maids answered the door and lead Jeezy over to the oversized sitting room where Montana entertained his guest. As soon as Jeezy stepped foot in the sitting area the smile he had on his face quickly turned into a frown. On the couch he saw a man that went by the name Big Tone. In the past, Big Tone and Jeezy had several altercations with one another. The altercations never got physical, but the two men still didn't care for each other. Big Tone hated the fact that Montana had always fronted Jeezy work and made him pay for his. In Big Tone's mind it was Jeezy who was in his way and stopping him from growing. Big Tone was a big man he weighed 250 pounds and was as strong as an ox. He sat slouched down on the couch with a smirk on his face. The big man wore way more jewelry then he needed, but showing off was what Big Tone did best.

Jeezy walked in and greeted Big Tone with a simple head nod. Big Tone returned the gesture. Jeezy thumbed through his iPhone as he waited for Montana to enter the sitting area. Three minutes later Montana entered the sitting area with a glass of wine in one hand and a cigar in the other.
"Jeezy, Big Tone it's great to see you two," he said with a smile. "Would y'all like something to drink?"

"No thank you" Jeezy declined. "I can't really chat for long. I need my usual and I'mma get going. I gotta get back on my feet." Jeezy wasn't in a rush, but he didn't want to hang around Montana while Big Tone was present.

"We need to talk" Montana said taking a sip from his wine. "I'm afraid I can't sell you anymore work at this time."

"Why not" Jeezy asked confused?

"You too hot right now. I think you may need to take a little time off until some of this heat dies down" Montana told him. "This heat you got on you is bad for business. I'm sure you understand."

"Too much heat" Jeezy echoed? "My fiancé is sitting up in a jail cell right now and the FEDS took my house and whatever they missed the lawyer took. I need this please! You know I've never come up short or made one payment late. Look out for me this one time."

"No can do" Montana said sternly. "Business is business and this ain't personal Jeezy. This is business" he told him. "Once this heat dies down then come back and we'll see what we can work out."

Jeezy shook his head in disgust. "All this money out here and you ready to let it go to waste just because my house got raided?"

Montana laughed. "I'm not letting any money go to waste. Big Tone here is going to pick right up where you left off."

"I'm going to show you how to get it done and get it done right." Big Tone stood to his feet with a smile on his face. This was the moment he had been waiting for. Now that it was here it was no way he was going to fuck this up. "Stupid clowns like you don't know shit about hustling. Amateurs like you lead the FEDS straight to your front door then wonder why you sitting in jail looking stupid."

"I wasn't even talking to your fat ass" Jeezy capped back. "Keep my name out of your mouth or else its going to be some problems" he warned.

Big Tone laughed loudly. "Nigga please" he said walking towards Jeezy. "You are talking tough for a nigga that would rather his girl go to jail instead of him. You better go talk that tough shit to somebody else!"

The two men stood face to face sizing one another up. Jeezy so badly wanted to smack Big Tone's soul out of his body, but he knew if he disrespected Montana's house he would have a bigger problem on his hands and at the time Jeezy didn't need any more problems.

"Do something" Big Tone challenged.

"Y'all two chill out and don't disrespect my house" Montana told them.

"I'm gonna see you again" Jeezy smirked as he turned and exited Montana's house.

"I can't stand that mufucka" Big Tone said once Jeezy was gone. "I don't know why you don't let me kill that clown."

"We shouldn't have to worry about him anymore" Montana said. "He's got more than enough problems to deal with. You just focus on getting this money."

Big Tone had left the conversation at that, but in his mind he told himself that the next time he ran into Jeezy he was going to put him in his place for trying to talk tough like he was built like that.

When Jeezy got back inside his car he was smoking mad. He couldn't believe how Montana was treating him; just because his house had been raided. Montana not giving Jeezy no work cause of the heat was basically like telling Jeezy he wasn't giving him no work cause if he got locked up he thought Jeezy might would have snitched. The more Jeezy thought about it the angrier he became.

The BMW tires screeched as Jeezy pulled away from the driveway. As Jeezy rode back to hotel he listened to Fabolous' new album as he thought about what his next move was going to be. He didn't have a clue how he was going to make money or where to start. Jeezy knew if he got some work from someone other than Montana that the quality wouldn't be able to compare to the quality of work that Montana was supplying. Jeezy always played things low key so he didn't have a big team or a lot of unnecessary niggas that he dealt with. He figured if he worked alone he couldn't snitch on himself.

Back in his hotel room Jeezy had a few drinks as he thought about his next move. His thoughts kept getting interrupted as flashes of him fucking Big Tone up kept on popping in his head.

"I got to get up outta here" Jeezy said to himself as he grabbed his keys and 40 caliber off the bed and headed out the door. Jeezy hopped in his BMW and just drove. He didn't have anywhere in particular he was going, but if he stayed in that room any longer he was going to go crazy.

As Jeezy cruised the streets he ran across a strip club that seemed like it was popping. He quickly pulled his BMW into the parking lot. Jeezy placed his 40 caliber under his seat as he hopped out and headed towards the entrance of the strip club. After a quick pat down the big bouncer allowed Jeezy to enter the strip club. Jeezy stepped in the strip club and immediately he was in a better mood. He needed something to take his mind off of his problems and this was the perfect distraction. A new Rick Ross song blared through the speakers as Jeezy made his way over to the bar. He ordered a bottle of Coconut Ciroc and asked for a hundred singles.

Jeezy tossed out a few singles as he watched and enjoyed the show that the strippers put on. Jeezy's body was in the strip club, but his mind was wondering what Paige was doing right now. He hoped that her little vacation would be a smooth one. Jeezy's thoughts were interrupted when a sexy light skin stripper approached him.

"All this ass in here shaking and your mind is on another planet." The stripper smiled. "What you over here thinking about?"

Jeezy smiled at the woman's forwardness. "What are you a therapist or something?"

"I could be your therapist" the stripper said brushing her exposed breast up against Jeezy as she leaned close to his ear. "Can I drink with you?"

"What's your name" Jeezy asked as he poured the woman a drink?
"Everyone calls me Pink" the stripper said while extending her hand.
"Jeezy" he said to her as the two shook hands.

Pink sized Jeezy up and liked what she was seeing. She could tell he wasn't like the rest of the perverts that entered the club on a night in and night out basis. Something about him was different.

"Shouldn't you be grinding up on one of these johns" Jeezy chuckled. "Don't let me stop your money baby."

"Never that" Pink said looking at Jeezy like he was insane. "If it's one thing you need to know about Pink, it's that she's going to always get that money" she said as she began popping one ass cheek at a time in front of Jeezy's face. Jeezy smiled as he sprinkled a few singles on Pink's back as he continued to watch her do her thing. The way Pink was popping her pussy and moving her body, Jeezy could tell that in the bedroom she wasn't anything to play with.

"Don't be scared. You can smack it if you want." Pink seductively leaned back and said in Jeezy's ear. Jeezy smirked as he tossed a few more singles on top of Pink's body. Pink smiled when she felt Jeezy smacking her ass. Pink favored the actress Lisa Ray except her hair was red.

"That's all you get for now" Pink smirked as she walked off leaving Jeezy with something to think about. She was feeling him, but she kept telling herself that a man that fine had to have a woman at home and Pink wasn't into sharing. She looked back and winked at Jeezy as she hopped up on the stage and began working the pole.

Jeezy smirked as he watched Pink work the pole like a professional. He liked how she moved, but she didn't have anything on Paige. His mind kept wondering back to his fiancé. He couldn't believe that she would be gone for three years. It just didn't seem real. He could still picture the wild sex they had the night before, that lead into the morning. Jeezy took a few more swigs from his bottle as he got up and headed towards the exit. He was enjoying watching the strippers shake their ass for cash, but he had to figure out how he was going to get some money. He needed a new gig bad. Right before Jeezy reached the exit he felt someone grab his shoulder. Jeezy turned around with the reflexes of a cat ready to attack. He calmed down when he saw it was just Pink.

"Damn you almost got laid out, running up on me like that" he laughed.

"Sorry" Pink said returning his stare. "You are leaving already?"

"Yeah, I wish I could just hang around the strip club all day" Jeezy said.

"Before you leave you wouldn't happen to have any E pills on you would you" Pink asked?

"Nah, why you be popping" he asked?

"Nah not me, but all these clowns in here do. Not to mention all these stripper bitches in here. Okay well sorry to hold you up" Pink said as she spun around until Jeezy stopped her.

"Mufucka's be rolling in here like that" Jeezy asked with a surprised look on his face?

"All day and all night" Pink told him.
"What time you get off?"

"In an hour." "Why, what's up" Pink asked?

"I wanna talk some business with you" Jeezy smiled. "I'mma be in the BMW parked out front."

"See you in an hour" Pink said in a sexually charged voice as she spun on her heels and headed back towards the stage. Jeezy watched as her ass jiggled with each step she took. He watched how every man in the strip clubs eyes were glued to her. Jeezy smiled as he walked to his BMW and waited until Pink got off the clock.

As Jeezy sat in his BMW waiting, he pulled out his iPhone and thumbed through a few pictures of him and Paige together. He made sure he took plenty of naked pictures of her before she turned herself in so he could please himself to them while she was gone. An hour later Jeezy saw a silver Audi A8 pull up on the side of him. When the driver's window rolled down, he saw Pink sitting behind the wheel. "My place or yours" she asked?

"Yours" Jeezy answered quickly. It was no way he was bringing her to his hotel room. For all he knew she could have been trying to set him up. He placed the gear in drive as he followed the Audi out the parking lot. Thirty minutes later Jeezy watched as the Audi pulled up in the drive way of a big expensive looking house. Jeezy hopped out his BMW and smiled as he looked up at the house. He loved to see a woman with her own shit. Pink stepped out the Audi dressed in an all white business suit with a pair of white four inch heels on to match.

"Can you grab my duffle bag from out the back seat for me please?"

"Damn" Jeezy huffed as he picked up the heavy bag. "Fuck you got up in here a dead body?"

Pink laughed as she opened the front door and stepped inside.
"Nah those are my different stage outfits and heels in there."

"You live here alone" Jeezy asked admiring Pink's house? He thought his and Paige's house was nice, but Pink's house made theirs look like an apartment.

"Yup all by myself" Pink said as she kicked off her heels and walked over to the kitchen. "Make yourself at home."

Jeezy sat on the leather couch and wondered how she could afford such a nice house like this off of a stripper's salary. She had to do something else on the side he thought. Pink returned back from the kitchen carrying two wine glasses and a bottle of Grey Goose.

"So what's on your mind" she said pouring them both a drink.

"I got a business proposition for you" Jeezy began. "If I can supply you an unlimited supply of E pills, would you be willing to sell them for me?"

"What's the split?" Pink took a slow sip from her glass.

"50/50" Jeezy explained. "I want you to be my partner."

Pink smiled. "I'm with it. More is always better."
"I don't mean any disrespect, but do you do more than dance at that club?" Jeezy asked curiously.

Pink looked at him like he was insane. "Are you asking me if I sell my ass at the club?"

"Not like that." Jeezy tried to down play it. "I mean I see this nice house and I feel if we are going to be partners, I need to know a few things about you" he said honestly.

"Well no I don't and have never sold my pussy" Pink said feeling slightly offended.

"I didn't mean any disrespect by that" Jeezy apologized. "Do you do anything on the side?"

"Yes I have several strippers who turn tricks for me" Pink told him.

"What you mean by turn tricks?"

"They sell their body and bring me the money and I give them a cut of whatever it is that they make at the end of the night" Pink explained.

"Why would them hoes sell their ass all night and then give you the money?" Jeezy didn't understand.

"The bitches I got under me, I brought them in off the street when they didn't have a pot to piss in." Pink went on. "It's only right that they break me off a little something."

Jeezy smiled. "So you a true business woman I see."
"That's enough about me." Pink sipped some more. "Tell me a little bit about yourself."

Jeezy took a sip from his glass before he spoke. "Recently my house got raided by the FEDS and today my fiancé took the charge for me." He went on to tell her a little bit about his past, but only what he wanted or needed her to know. For the rest of the night Jeezy and Pink got drunk while getting to know each other better until they both passed out on the couch.

Lock Down

Paige and eight other female inmates entered the dorm in a single line. Three C.O.'s escorted them through the dorm and called out each new inmate's bed number. When Paige heard her name called, the C.O. told her that her bunk number was 12 and on top.

As Paige walked through the aisles looking for her bed, she walked past a gang of rough looking bitches in the process. She kept her head held high as she walked confidently until she reached bed 12.

A big rough looking chick rested on the bottom bunk reading a book titled "Tears Of A Hustler". When she saw Paige standing, she quickly stood to her feet. "Listen" the big woman began in a nasty tone. "You up on the top bunk and I keep a clean cube. If you are a nasty bitch then we are gone have some problems."

Paige ignored the woman and sat her sheets and blanket on the top bunk. She smelled a foul odor coming from somewhere. When Paige looked down she spotted the big chick's jail issued boots leaning to the side. "Damn" Paige said to herself as she turned up her nose. This was her first day in the federal facility and she could already tell that this was going to be a long bid.

"Oh, and another thing" the big chick said. "If I catch you in my shit, I'm gonna wear your ass out!"

Paige shook her head as she lay on her bunk staring up at the ceiling. At that very moment she wondered what Jeezy was doing. She told herself that she wouldn't stress herself wondering what Jeezy was out on the streets doing. Without trust there was no relationship. "Fuck this shit" Paige said as she got up and grabbed her towel and headed for the shower. She stood directly under the shower head and let the hot water massage her face and scalp. It had been a week since the last time Paige had taken a shower. The hot water splashing off of her skin felt great. Since this was going to be Paige's new home for the next few years, she figured she might as well get used to this place so she started with a nice hot shower. After scrubbing her body clean for thirty minutes Paige cut the water off and dried her face with her wash rag. When she turned around, she saw two rough looking chicks standing there staring at her with lust in their eyes.

"Mmm...mmm...mmm!" One of the women hummed as she smiled. "Now that's what a woman should look like" she said giving her partner five.

Off the bat Paige knew the two women were dikes. She quickly snatched her towel off the rail and covered her body with it.

"What's your name" the woman asked?

"Paige."

"Well I'm Roxy and this here is Shawn" she said nodding to her partner.

"Nice to meet y'all" Paige said politely. She tried to play it cool, but inside she knew both of the women who stood before her were gay and right now she was looking like fresh meat.

"Is it really nice to meet me" Roxy said in a low sexy voice as she and Shawn moved in closer?
"Please" Paige begged. "Whatever yall plan on doing please don't. I don't want no trouble."

"As long as you give up that sweet pussy you won't have any trouble" Roxy said as she tugged at the bottom of Paige's towel.

Paige snatched her towel out of Roxy's grip as she backed up until her back hit the wall.

"Don't fight it baby" Roxy smiled. "You gon be my bitch" she said as she stroked Paige's hair. "Oh and we going to have a lot of fun together" she said flicking her tongue like a snake.

Paige swallowed hard as she balled up her fist. She wasn't just going to sit there and let the two dike bitches just have their way with her. If they wanted her pussy then they were going to have to fight for it. Just as Paige got ready to swing she noticed a female C.O. enter the shower room.

"Is everything alright in here" the C.O. asked suspiciously eyeing Roxy and Shawn?

"Yeah everything is fine" Roxy answered quickly.

"I wasn't talking to you mufucka" the C.O. growled! "I was talking to the new girl."

"Yes I'm fine" Paige said as she exited the shower room and headed back to her bunk. When she reached her bunk she saw her bunky eating some Oodles of Noodles and tuna fish. Paige turned up her nose as she quickly put her clothes back on and hopped back up on her bed. As she lay on her bunk she noticed Roxy and Shawn walking through the dorm undressing her with their eyes.

"On the chow" a C.O. yelled. Paige hopped off her bunk and got in a single file line with the rest of the women inmates and headed down to the mess hall.

"I hope they are serving something good today" the chick who stood behind Paige said. When Paige reached the mess hall it was filled with other women inmates already eating. As she waited in line to receive her food, she still couldn't believe that she was really in jail. It all felt like a dream to her; not a dream but a nightmare. When Paige stepped up to the counter with her food tray the inmates who served the food tossed two slices of bread on her tray. As she went down the line, another inmate food server slapped a scoop of mashed potatoes down on her tray and last but not least a piece of meat that looked like a burger patty was placed on her tray. When Paige sat down she picked over her food while all the other girls dug into their food as if it was a meal from a 5 star restaurant.

"This bitch must think she's too good to eat this food" an inmate wearing a du-rag commented.

"What are you talking about" Paige said looking at the girl? "Do I even know you?"

"No you don't know me and trust and believe you don't want to get to know me either" the woman threatened raising her voice!

Paige knew if she was going to survive in this kind of environment that she would have to smack the shit out of a few bitches and stoop down to their level. She had heard all the stories about what went down in jail, but she assumed the stories were exaggerated. Now she was finding out that not only were the stories real, but so were the female inmates.

"Just keep your eyes off my shit a'ight" Paige said looking the other chick in her eyes. Before Paige could see it coming the woman jumped across the table and clothes lined Paige out of her chair.

"OOOOOOH SHIT!" Another inmate cooed as the whole cafeteria gathered around to see what was going on.

The woman had a tight grip on Paige's long hair as she went to work on her with her free hand. Paige struggled to break the woman's grip from her hair, but it was no use. She swung and clawed as best she could until finally several C.O.'s came and separated the two.

"Bitch this shit ain't over with!" The woman yelled holding a few strands of Paige's hair in her hand. Paige was escorted back to her dorm where she went without food for the rest of the night. For the entire night Paige just cried. No matter how bad she wanted to pick up and leave, she knew she was stuck there. This was only day one. Now she had 1,094 days left to go.

Two Months Later

Jeezy sat in the back of the strip club watching Pink handle her business. She worked the johns and other dancers in the club like a professional. For the past two months business had been booming thanks to Pink. She appeared out of nowhere and saved Jeezy's life. Jeezy was thankful to have Pink as a business partner, but on top of just being partners Jeezy was also Pink's protector. Any problems, Pink looked to Jeezy to handle them and that's what Jeezy did best.

Pink walked over and gave Jeezy a hug and slipped a hand full of cash in his hands on the low. "Shit popping in here tonight."

Jeezy pulled Pink down onto his lap so the two blended in with the rest of the crowd. "Tell me about it" he said discreetly slipping the money in his pocket.

"You see that African nigga over there in the cut" Pink asked gyrating her hips to the beat that blasted through the speaker?

"That clown over there in the suit" Jeezy asked looking over in the African's direction. He saw an African man sitting all alone tossing plenty of money in the air as he watched it rain down on the strippers.

"He's coked up out of his mind and spending money like its water" Pink told him.

"Think this risk will be worth the reward" he asked taking one more look over at the African man?

"No doubt" Pink answered with a smile. She knew a come up when she saw it and the African was just that, a quick come up.

"Fuck it." "I'm on it" Jeezy said downing the rest of his drink in one gulp.

Pink walked past the African man and he quickly grabbed her wrist. "You are so beautiful. Why on earth are you in here belittling yourself?"

"Being beautiful doesn't pay the bills" Pink replied.

"If you were my woman you wouldn't want or need for anything. In my country you would get treated like royalty" the African said as he kissed the back of Pink's hand.

"I mean that sounds cool and all that, but I don't think I'll be going to the motherland anytime soon" she said as she turned to walk away.

"Wait" he said grabbing her wrist again. "Please stay with me for the night."

"Nah." "I don't think so" Pink declined.

"Name your price" the African man smiled. He knew American woman did anything in the name of the old mighty dollar and he had to have Pink.

"$10,000" Pink said waiting for a response.
"Done" the African man said as if she had said two dollars.

"Up front" Pink said with her hand out. For some reason she didn't trust the man.

"Not a problem" the African man said as he stood to his feet. "My limo is parked out front. Go change your clothes and meet me out front. That's where the money is."

"I'll be out in twenty minutes baby." Pink smiled as she disappeared in the back.

Jeezy sat in the cut as he watched the African man exit the club. He quickly stood to his feet and did the same thing. When Jeezy made it outside he saw the African man hop in an all black limousine. He quickly made his way over to his BMW and grabbed his 40 caliber from under the seat and his hoodie from out the back seat. "Here we go" Jeezy said to himself as he threw the hoodie over his head and headed towards the limo.

The African man sat in the back of the limo counting out $10,000. He didn't have a problem paying for the finer things in life. When the limo door flung open the African thought it was Pink entering. His eyes almost popped out his head when he saw the big gun in his face. Seconds later Pink hopped in the front seat with her .380 pointed at the driver's head. "Drive" she told him.

"What's going on here" the African asked in a heavy accent?

"Shut the fuck up" Jeezy huffed snatching the $10,000 from his hands! "Where's the rest of the money?"

"You are making a big mistake." If you leave now I promise, I will forget about everything and you won't have to deal with the consequences later" the African said in a calm tone. WAK!

Jeezy smacked the African across the face with his gun. "Last time I'm asking you. Where's the rest of the money?"
The African man smiled before he replied. "It's in the trunk."
"Pull this mufucka over" Pink ordered. The limo driver quickly did as he was told.

"Pop the trunk" Jeezy ordered as he hopped out and made his way to the trunk. When Jeezy hopped out the limo, Pink aimed her gun at the African's head.

"I'm a very, very wealthy and powerful man in my country" he said. "I promise you, you will be hearing from me and my people again."

Pink didn't reply. It was no need because she held the gun which meant it was she who was in control. She just looked at the African man and smiled.

"It's all here" Jeezy said as he leaned his head back in the limo. "Come on let's go."
"Are you crazy" Pink yelled! "He has seen our faces we have to kill him!"

Jeezy thought about it for a second and she was right. Not only did he see their faces, but he also knew where Pink worked. Jeezy quickly raised his arm and pulled the trigger. Pink watched as the African's brains splattered all over the back window.

"Do the driver so we can get out of here" Jeezy said in a hurried voice. Pink aimed her .380 at the driver's head and paused for a few second before she finally pulled the trigger taking the innocent man's life.

"Come on we gotta go" Jeezy said as he helped Pink up out of the limo. The two jogged down the street and quickly flagged down a cab. "The London hotel" Jeezy told the cab driver. He noticed that Pink wasn't shaken up and seemed unmoved about the whole situation. He didn't say anything because he figured she must have killed before.

"What?" Pink asked noticing Jeezy looking at her.

"Nothing you just seem a little too calm" Jeezy pointed out.

"It was either him or us." "I did what I had to do" Pink said as if it was no big deal. In her mind she felt like if the tables were reversed the African would have did the same to her so why not do it to him? Jeezy paid the cab driver as he and Pink entered the London hotel. The two hurried over to the elevators and hopped on one.

"Do you think they noticed the blood on my shirt" Pink asked looking down at her shirt?

"I hope not" Jeezy answered quickly as they walked down the hall to his room.

"So this is where you've been living" Pink asked as she stepped through the door?

"Gotta do what I gotta do" Jeezy answered as he turned the duffle bag upside down and watched the piles of money fall on the bed. He looked over at Pink and smiled.

"Do I know how to pick 'em or what?" Pink laughed loudly as she poured her and Jeezy a drink. The next hour the two spent counting up the money they had just lifted from the

African man. At the end of their counting, Jeezy and Pink had $180,000 to split between the two of them.

"What you gone do with your half" Pink asked as she removed her bloody shirt and bra as she lay down on the bed letting her breast hang freely?

"Saving mines" Jeezy replied.

"Oh you saving for the big wedding you're having in three years right?"

"Not only that, but I don't even have a place to live" Jeezy told her. "I'm tired of living out of a room. This shit is whack. I'mma probably get me a one bedroom apartment just so I can have somewhere to rest my head."

"It ain't no way I'mma let you be living in some dirty apartment when I got that big ass house that I live in all alone" Pink told him.

"I'm saying I don't wanna be invading nobody's space or nothing like that." Jeezy knew she probably had several men that she dealt with and didn't want to mess nothing up for her. Plus he was the type who always had to have his own for just in case reasons.

"Okay well just think about it" Pink said as she hopped off the bed and headed for the bathroom so she could take a shower. As Jeezy sat on the bed, he wondered what Paige was doing at that moment and wondered if she was alright. He knew she was a strong woman and would be able to survive jail, but he worried about her safety and well-being at times. Jeezy had spent time in prison in his past. He knew how hard it could be in there sometimes so he prayed that Paige stayed strong physically and most of all mentally. Jeezy's thoughts were interrupted when Pink came out of the bathroom butt naked.

"What you over here thinking about" Pink asked with a smile as she picked up her cup and sipped it slowly? She knew Jeezy was checking out her body and she loved the attention. Jeezy sighed loudly. "I got a lot on my mind right now."

Pink pushed Jeezy down on the bed and straddled him. "Anything I can do to take your mind off of your problems?"

"Come on I told you from the beginning I got a girl" Jeezy reminded her.

"I don't want to be your girl." "I just want some of this dick" Pink said massaging Jeezy's manhood through his jeans. She had been trying to downplay the feelings she had for him, but she could no longer control herself.

"Chill" Jeezy said putting up a weak protest. His mouth was saying no, but his dick was saying something else. Pink leaned down and sloppily kissed Jeezy in his mouth as she grabbed his hands and placed them on her soft firm breast. The two kissed sloppily as Jeezy's hands explored Pink's firm curves. Pink reached down and unbuckled Jeezy's belt. From how hard Jeezy's tool was she knew he wanted her just as bad as she wanted him. Just as Pink unbuckled his pants Jeezy's phone went off.

"Don't answer it baby" Pink said in a muffled voice as she kissed up and down his chest. Jeezy reached down and grabbed his phone and saw that the number was blocked which meant it was Paige calling.

"I gotta take this" he sat up and answered. "Hey baby what's up?"

Pink rolled her eyes as she got off of him, got dressed, and packed away her money.

"Nothing and I miss you so much" Paige said on the other line. "I wanna come home" she whined.

"I know baby I miss you too" Jeezy said fixing his pants. He felt bad about what had just happened, but he did his best to fight Pink off. "How are they treating you in there?"

"A bunch a bum bitches in here running they mouth all day" Paige huffed. "I don't know how people can go back and forth to jail like it's all fun and games."

"Well just know after this you will never have to see the inside of a jail ever again" Jeezy told her.

"How's everything going on the outside" Paige asked?

"On my grind" Jeezy replied as he noticed Pink packing up all of his belongings. "I'll be up there to see you sometime this week."

"I can't wait to see you" Paige said as she heard the operator on the phone notifying her that she only had 60 seconds remaining before the call would disconnect. "I guess that's my cue." "I love you so much baby please be good."

"I love you too baby and you know I'mma hold it down out here" Jeezy said just as the phone disconnected. Jeezy placed his phone back in its case as he watched Pink continue to pack up his things. "What you doing?"

"You're coming home with me" Pink said. "I'm not gone just sit around and let you live out of a hotel when I got a big ass house that I live in all by myself that's crazy."

Jeezy knew this was a bad idea for him to be moving in with Pink, but he figured he could save more money this way and it would be more convenient for him in the long run especially now that they were making such good money together. Jeezy helped Pink pack up the rest of his things as they went downstairs and caught a cab.

"We'll just pick up our cars tomorrow" Pink said with a smile when they arrived at her house. Instead of taking Jeezy's things to the guest room, Pink took them up to the master bedroom. Jeezy sat the rest of his things down in the living room and walked over to the kitchen to get him a drink. After everything that had went down he definitely needed a strong drink.

Jeezy sat down on the couch and turned on the TV when he heard his cell phone ringing. He looked down and saw Montana's name flashing across the screen. "Fuck outta here" he huffed as he hit the silent button on his phone and stuck it back down in its case. Whatever Montana was calling Jeezy about he didn't want to hear it. After how he had kicked Jeezy to the curb he had cut all ties with his former connect.

Twenty minutes later Pink returned back down to the living room butt naked. She walked up to the couch and stood directly in front of Jeezy. She cocked her leg up and planted it on the couch exposing her freshly waxed pussy. Pink reached down and guided Jeezy's head towards her pussy. As Jeezy's head got close he noticed that whatever she had put on smelled like cotton candy.

Jeezy firmly grabbed Pink's ass pushing her closer to his mouth as he sucked and licked all over her clit. Pink moaned loudly as she stood up on the couch and began riding Jeezy's face. She used a few of her stripper moves as she gyrated her ass and hips grinding her pussy all over Jeezy's face.

Jeezy then effortlessly flipped Pink upside down as he continued to eat her pussy like it was the last super. Pink moaned loudly as she pulled Jeezy's dick from out of his pants and began sucking on it nice and slow while she jerked it at the same time. After ten minutes of sucking, Jeezy could no longer take it anymore. He made Pink get on all fours on the plush carpet as he entered her from behind. Pink winced when she felt Jeezy enter her walls. Jeezy started off with slow strokes until he got into a nice rhythm.

"Ahhh...Ahhh" Pink moaned as she felt Jeezy spread both of her ass cheeks apart. "Tear this pussy up!"

"Argggggg" Jeezy groaned as he pulled out and released all over Pink's round ass. When it was all over Jeezy laid on his back feeling stupid. He felt as if he had betrayed Paige. Jeezy knew what Pink was up to, but he couldn't resist her for some reason.

"Damn that dick was so good." Pink smiled as she got up and went back upstairs leaving Jeezy downstairs to think about what had just happened.

In Too Deep

The next morning Jeezy was awaken by his ringing cell phone. He rolled over and saw Montana's name flashing across the screen again. "Yo what's good?"

"Wake up" Montana said. "Be at my place in half an hour." Before Jeezy could reply the line went dead in his ear. He sat his phone back down on the night stand and wondered what Montana wanted. Obviously it had to be something important since he wouldn't discuss it over the phone. Jeezy quickly got dressed, grabbed his 40 caliber and headed out the door. When Jeezy pulled his Benz up in front of Montana's house he saw several limos and expensive looking cars parked out front. He rang the doorbell and patiently waited. Seconds later, one of Montana's maids answered the door and lead Jeezy over to the sitting room. When Jeezy entered the sitting room he spotted Montana, Big Tone, and a bunch of African men sitting around with angry looks on their faces.

"So glad you could make it." Montana greeted Jeezy with a hand shake. "We have a big problem on our hands." "One of my African associates was murdered last night and I just wanted to know if you heard anything about it out in the streets."

"Nah I ain't hear nothing about any African" Jeezy lied with a straight face. Once he saw the whole room full of rich African men he knew he had fucked up, but he still had to play it cool. "This African must have been a heavy hitter in his country."

"Yeah he was the real deal" Montana said. "85% of the dope in the United States came from him and his people."

"Damn that's crazy" Jeezy said. "What was he doing up in the city anyway?"

"Tricking" Montana answered quickly. "Oscar loved American women and mainly strippers" Montana said as he handed Jeezy a photo of Oscar. "Keep your ear to the streets and let me know if you hear anything." "My friends here are willing to pay big money to whoever can lead us to Oscar's murderers." He paused to take a sip from his drink. "I heard it may have been The Gambino Brothers."

"Who the fuck is that" Jeezy asked?

"These two ruthless ass brothers who will rob anything and anybody under the sun" Montana said. "We are not sure if it's them yet, but this has their name written all over it."

"I never heard of any Gambino Brothers."

"They are two cold blooded killers with nothing to lose." "They got plenty of money and they just rob mufucka's for the hell of it." Montana shook his head.

"Black or Spanish?"

"Spanish, Mexican what difference does it make" Montana replied.

"I'll keep my eyes and ears open" Jeezy said with a head nod as he noticed Big Tone staring him down.

"Thanks Jeezy, I appreciate it" Montana said as he walked Jeezy to the door.

Once outside, Jeezy walked swiftly back to his Benz. He pounded his fist on the steering wheel out of frustration. He had really fucked up bad. He knew it would only be a matter of time before the Africans connected him to the murder. He was going to have to figure out something and figure something out fast.

Once back at the house Jeezy walked out to the back where the pool was and spotted Pink along with three other women in the pool getting drunk and listening to Drake's new CD.

"Hey baby" Pink sang happily. "Come get in." "The water is warm."

"Not right now" Jeezy said dismissing the idea. "I need to speak to you inside for a second."

Pink hopped out the pool butt naked with a wine glass in her hand as she walked dripping wet into the kitchen. "What's wrong baby?"

"The African nigga we killed just so happened to be connected." Jeezy shook his head.

"He was a Made-Man" Pink asked?

"Yeah" Jeezy sighed. "And he's got an army of African mufuckas out looking for the ones who murdered him."

"Fuck them Africans." Pink flicked her hand dismissively. "Anybody could have killed that clown." "We covered our tracks so you ain't got anything to worry about" she said as she kissed Jeezy on the lips.

"Now come join me and my friends in the pool."

"Who are them bitches?" Jeezy asked taking a peek out the back door at the three beautiful women splashing around in the water.

"Those are my best three workers" Pink smiled. "They each bring in at least $5,000 a week and that's not counting what they bring in with the pills." "I told them all about you and they are dying to meet you." She winked as she walked back outside and slipped back in the pool.

"Fuck it" Jeezy said as he stripped down butt naked and made his way over to the pool. He sat at the edge of the pool and let his legs dangle in the water. Pink quickly gave her girls a head nod and watched as they surrounded Jeezy like a pack of wolves. Jeezy smiled as two of the girls gave him head while the other one licked and sucked all over his balls. Pink sat back and looked on. In her mind Jeezy was now her man and nothing pleased her more than to see her man happy.

All Eyes on Me

Paige reached the package room and waited in the long line of inmates until her name was called. The women waiting for packages were the fortunate ones and all the other inmates were less fortunate. As Paige stood in the line, she thanked God that she had someone on the outside who loved her dearly. Paige had sent Jeezy a list of all of the things that she needed in a letter and three days later she was standing in the package room. When the C.O. called Paige's name she quickly stepped up and watched as the C.O. searched through her food and snacks as if it held a bomb inside. Paige sighed loudly as she watched the C.O. fish through the bras and panties that Jeezy sent her.

"Damn" Paige huffed. "How many times you going to check my draws acting like you never saw a thong before."

"Listen here you cunt bitch" the C.O. said jabbing his index finger through the air in Paige's direction. "I'll check this shit as many times as I fucking feel like it. You got a problem with that? I didn't think so" he said nastily answering his own question.

Paige wasn't racist, nor did she have a problem with white people, but how the racist C.O.'s treated the inmates made her sick to her stomach. The white C.O.'s treated all of the black inmates like they were animals and as if they never made a mistake in their lives or broke or bent any laws. Paige decided her best bet was to just be quiet and patiently wait until the old racist white man finished searching through her things for the thousandth time. After searching Paige's package three more times just to fuck with her, the C.O. finally released the package to her. Paige sucked her teeth as she snatched the clear see through bag and headed back towards her dorm. As Paige strolled back to her dorm she could already taste the good food that Jeezy had sent her. Even though the only appliances available to her were a hot pot and a microwave, Paige knew how to make something out of nothing in a kitchen. If it was one thing Paige knew, it was how to cook. She had been cooking all of her life. Paige entered the dorm and instantly all eyes were on her and her bag full of goodies. All of the unfortunate inmates eyed Paige's bag full of real food with hungry looks in their eyes.

"Fuck that" Paige said to herself. "I ain't sharing shit."
When Paige reached her cubical, her bunky quickly sat up with a smile on her face. "Yeah; we eating tonight" she said rubbing her hands together. "What we got?"

Paige looked at the big bitch like she was crazy. "WE ain't got shit!" she said putting an emphasis on the word we.

The big chick quickly put her boots on and tied them up tight.

"This my mufucking spot" she pointed at her chest, "and if you bring some food up in here we both eating!"

"Humph" Paige sighed. "I ain't got anything for you. You ain't said two words to me since I got here and now that I got some food you wanna speak. Fuck outta here!"

Before the words could fully leave Paige's mouth, Big Momma had snuffed her. The impact from the blow caused Paige to take a few steps backwards.

"Bitch play the bathroom!" Big Momma barked as she stormed off to the bathroom.

Paige held on to her face. For a second she couldn't believe that her bunky had sucker punched her over some food that wasn't even hers. She took a second to regroup before she headed to the bathroom. Paige wasn't a big fighter, but she wasn't going to sit around and let another bitch just punch her in her face and get away with it.

Paige entered the bathroom and saw Big Momma standing in the middle of the floor wearing the facility issued pants and an all black sports bra. "Come on bitch let's go" she growled!

Paige swallowed hard as she stepped up and swung on Big Momma. Paige went blow for blow with the much bigger woman for as long as she could. Eventually Big Momma grabbed a tight hold of Paige's long hair and flung her down to the floor. Paige blocked her face as best she could as she felt the powerful punches rain in. At that moment all Paige could do was kick her legs wildly as she fought for her life.

After pounding on Paige like she was a child Big Momma felt as if her bunky had, had enough. "Next time I ask for something, you better set that out" she snarled giving Paige one last kick to her face.

Paige peeled herself up off the floor and stood over the sink looking at her battered face in the mirror. The reflection that looked back at her instantly brought tears to her eyes.

"How the fuck did my life get like this?" She said to herself as she wiped the tears from her face.

"Here you go" a voice said from her left. Paige turned around and saw another inmate standing there holding a rag in her hand.

"Here clean yourself up" the other chick said handing Paige the rag.

"Thanks" Paige said accepting the rag. As she fixed her face she watched the other chick through the mirror and noticed that she was a bit older than her. "So what's your story" Paige asked? "You must want something."

"Why would you say that?" The chick asked sitting on the edge of the sink next to Paige.

"People in here only speak if they want something" Paige chuckled.

"Well I don't want anything from you sweetie and my name is Rose" the chick said extending her hand. Paige looked down at Rose's hand and continued to clean her face. "I'm Paige."

"Listen I been in here for ten years" Rose said, "and those bitches ain't gone stop fucking with you unless you stab one of them bitches!"

"But why me though? I haven't done anything to anyone" Paige said confused. She couldn't understand why these women would rather tear her down instead of embrace her.

"Because you not like the rest of us" Rose chuckled. "You don't know what it's to struggle and you were raised with a silver spoon in your mouth. They can't stand to see these fake ass high class bitches walking around here with their nose up in the air."

"So it's my fault that I did something with my life or that I wanted more out of life than to be living in a housing project?"

"It may sound crazy but that's how it works in here. They don't mind taking from you because they know you can easily get more" Rose explained.

"So let me get this right" Paige paused taking a second to take in and process what Rose had just explained to her. "So they gone keep fucking with me just because I decided to do something with my life?"

"Basically" Rose replied.

"Well I ain't stabbing anybody over some food" Paige huffed. "That's just crazy and ignorant" she said as she stormed out the bathroom. She couldn't believe she had just had a fight over her own shit. Paige couldn't understand why the women acted so rough and violent. If they were smart they would be nice to her and maybe when they were released she might look out for them and try to help them get a job or even try to hook them up with a nice man.

When Paige reached her bunk she saw Roxy, Tammy, and Big Momma all in her cube eating up all of the snacks and food that Jeezy had brought for her.

"Hey baby" Roxy said with a smirk on her face. "You ready to come home to daddy? If you were my bitch nobody would fuck with you!"

Paige ignored the dike's comments as she went to reach for her bag of goodies. Tammy quickly snatched the bag from Paige's hands. "Bitch don't touch our shit!"

Paige wanted to punch that gay bitch in her face, but she couldn't take another beating; especially a three on one.

Roxy and Tammy slapped hands with Big Momma as they left the cube with all of Paige's belongings.

"I'll see you later baby" Roxy whispered in Paige's ear as she smacked her on the ass.

Paige stood in the middle of her cube looking stupid. Not only did she get her ass whipped, but she also was back to square one. Now she needed more food and under clothes. She slowly climbed up on her bunk and stared up at the ceiling and cried silently. She so badly wanted to go home and lay in Jeezy's arms. Whenever Paige had a bad day she could always rely on Jeezy to make everything better, but now that she was locked up Jeezy seemed so far away. Sometimes it felt like she was never going to be able to go back home. Right now all Paige could do was pray and hope that the rest of her stay would be better than the way it started.

***

Pink's Christian Louboutin red bottom heels click-clacked loudly on the hardwood floor as she made her way over to the bar area where Jeezy sat sipping on a glass of Ciroc. Out of the twenty-nine years of living on earth Pink had never had a man who treated and talked to her the way she deserved to be treated and talked to. She was quickly falling in love with Jeezy. She loved the fact that she could talk to him about anything no matter how big or small it was. Another thing Pink loved about Jeezy was his hustle. Rain, sleet, or snow Jeezy was on his grind.

"So how many niggas your girls said gone be in the house?" Jeezy asked going over the plan in his head.

"Three" Pink answered. "They said it's always the same three men. Why, what's wrong baby?"

"I'm still thinking about them African's mufuckas" Jeezy said honestly. For some reason in his heart he felt like the Africans were going to somehow find out it was him who was responsible for the murder and track him down.

"Stop worrying about that shit" Pink said rubbing his back. "That shit happened four months ago. When are you going to let it go?"

"Sorry" Jeezy apologized.

"Besides you said it yourself that they think it was the Gambino Brothers. So fuck it. Let them think what they wanna think" Pink said. "I need you focused for tonight okay baby?" She said leaning in and kissing Jeezy on the lips. Pink's girls had set up a nice lick for tonight and if they were going to pull it off she was going to need Jeezy to be at his best. "I'm going to go change my clothes" Pink said as she walked off.

As Jeezy sat at the counter he began thinking about Paige. His plan was to make as much money as he could until Paige was released from prison. Once she was released, he planned on spending as much time with her as he could. He also planned to help get Paige back on the right track as far as her acting career was concerned. Ten minutes later Pink returned back downstairs wearing all black just like Jeezy.

"Let's do this" Jeezy said as he handed Pink a 45. Outside the two hopped in a stolen Acura that Jeezy had stolen earlier and pulled out of the garage. For the entire ride Jeezy and Pink were silent as they enjoyed the sounds of Fabulous' new CD. Jeezy pulled up a block away from the destination and kept the engine running. He reached in the back seat and removed a Tech-9. The two covered their heads with a skully and the bottom of their faces with a black bandana.

Jeezy walked up to the front door and shot the lock off. He then quickly raised his leg and kicked the door open. BOOM! Pink was the first one inside the house. She entered the living room and saw a six person orgy going on. She raised her 45 and fired a single shot into the ceiling. "Nobody fucking move", she yelled! The three victims looked up in shock like a deer caught in headlights.

"Tie them mufuckas up" Jeezy ordered as he kept his Tech-9 trained on the trio. After a thirty minute search of the house Pink found the stash.

"Come on let's get up outta here" Jeezy said as he headed for the exit. Just as he reached the door he heard three loud thunderous gunshots go off. POW! POW! POW!

When Jeezy turned around he saw Pink standing over the three men holding a smoking gun in her hand. He quickly walked over to Pink and roughly forced her back up against the wall. "What the fuck is wrong with you!" Jeezy yelled in her face. "Why did you do that?"

"They saw my girl's faces" Pink countered. "They would have easily tracked us down so I did what I had to do."
Jeezy raised his fist and shook his head as he put it back down. "Let's go!"

"What? I had to baby." Pink explained, "If they tracked my girls down, they would have given us up and you know it."

Jeezy roughly grabbed Pink by her arm and forced her back up again the car. "We were supposed to rob these guys, not murder them!" He yelled in a harsh whisper, "The shit you doing will get us put in jail forever; forever!"

"I'm sorry baby" Pink said with her head hung low. "I was just trying to make sure we covered our tracks. That's all."

Jeezy sighed loudly. "Get in the car" he said as he walked over to the other three girls who sat in the brown minivan. "I'mma need y'all to go back in there and wipe down everything yall touched and if yall smoked anything take the clips out of the ashtray. If yall drank anything, take the glasses yall drank from. If anything happens, I don't know yall."

"And we don't know you" the three girls all said together!

Jeezy hopped back in the stolen car and gunned the engine. For the whole ride back home Pink apologized for what she had done. In her mind she thought she was doing the right thing. If it meant taking a few lives to save her own, then so be it. If it ever came down to killing someone to save her own or Jeezy's life Pink wouldn't hesitate to pull the trigger. Jeezy pulled over on a deserted block and hopped out the stolen car. He grabbed the duffle bag filled with money and tossed it around his neck. He and Pink walked down a few blocks and flagged down a cab.

When they stepped inside the house Pink grabbed Jeezy and slid in his arms. "I'm sorry baby" she said. "I hate it when you're mad at me."

"I'm not mad. I just don't want to go to jail over some dumb shit" Jeezy told her.

"I was just thinking about us and our future" Pink whined.

"Our future?" Jeezy echoed. "Come on baby I already told you I'm engaged" he reminded her. "What we doing is cool and all that but I already told you what it was from the jump."

"No baby I wasn't saying our future like" Pink said trying to down play it. "I just don't want anything leading back to us. Hopefully the Gambino Brothers will take the rap for this robbery/murder as well" she chuckled.

Jeezy had heard stories about the Gambino Brothers, but never had he met anyone who claimed to know the brothers personally. In his mind he wondered if they really existed. "I understand what you saying, but at the same time we have to be cautious."

Pink smiled devilishly as she melted down to her knees and began unbuckling Jeezy's belt. Once Pink's lips wrapped around Jeezy's pole he'd forgotten what he was even complaining about.

Instead he grabbed the back of Pink's head and began fucking her mouth like it was a pussy. Pink moaned loudly as she let Jeezy have his way with her mouth until he finally came hard. Pink swallowed every last drop as she stood up and headed for the shower. "Round two is in the bedroom" she chimed when she reached the top of the steps and then disappeared into the bedroom. Jeezy stood in the middle of the living room with his pants down to his ankles with a puzzled look on his face. After a performance like that it was no way he could stay mad with Pink.

The Gambino Brothers

Alex Gambino and his young brother Victor Gambino sat in a motel enjoying the company of two young black prostitutes. Something they did often since their one rule was to never be involved with anyone intimately due to the nature of their occupation.

The Gambino Brothers would rob any and everything moving. If anyone ever got the drop on them the first thing they would do was go for their wives or close loved ones, but the Gambino Brothers had no love ones. Their mother had died from an overdose of heroin and they had killed their father in fear that when he found out what they were doing he was going to turn them in. Since day one, all the Gambino Brothers had were each other.

Alex being the older one of the two felt like it was his job to look after his younger brother Victor, but out of the two brothers Victor was the loose cannon. They both had enough money to retire and live the good life on a beach somewhere, but that wasn't what the Gambino Brothers were about. When someone spoke their names the first thing that came to mind was violence, murder, and destruction. Their motto was anybody could get it.

Being born and raised half of their lives in Mexico, the Gambino Brothers were no stranger to violence and poverty. They grew up rough and hard and they planned on dying that way.

Victor smiled as he watched the two ladies in front of him eat each other out. He loved to watch women on women action. It was something about it that turned him all the way on.

Alex stood and leaned against the wall nursing a drink as he watched the show from a distance. He loved women, but he didn't trust them. He and his brother Victor had used plenty of women in their day to help set their victims up. Alex smiled as he continued to watch the show until he saw several shadow figures outside the window walking past at a slow creep. He quickly grabbed his Mossberg pump shotgun that he always held close by.

Ever since Alex was a young boy his weapon of choice had always been the Mossberg shotgun. No man on earth could operate the gun better than him. Alex raised his shotgun and aimed it at the window and pulled the trigger. BOOM! Immediately both of the prostitutes screamed at the top of their lungs. Alex quickly cocked another round into the chamber and blew a hole through the front door. Seconds later the sound of automatic gun fire erupted throughout the motel room.

Victor quickly reached down and grabbed his twin 45's, and placed his back to wall with his two guns pointed directly at the front door. He smiled as he waited for the intruders to come inside. Victor glanced over at his brother and gave him a head nod. Alex quickly nodded back as several African men barged into the room. Victor opened fired dropping the men just as quickly as they entered. Once all the gunfire ended Alex and Victor slowly walked over all the dead bodies and examined them.

"Who the fuck would want us dead?" Victor chuckled stepping over the dead bodies.

"A lot of people" Alex said, "but I don't recall us fucking with no Africans." That's when he heard one of the intruders moaning and holding his bloody thigh. Alex quickly aimed his shotgun down at the man's head. "Who sent you?"

"Fuck you" the African man said in a heavy accent. Alex was getting ready to say something else, but lost his train of thought when Victor pumped two rounds in the man's leg.

"Okay, okay please don't shoot me no more!" The African man screamed out in pain.

"Who sent you?" Alex asked again.

"Montana" the African man squealed. "He wasn't about to give up his boss so he gave the killers the second best answer."

"Who the fuck is Montana?" Victor chimed in from the sideline, "and why does he want us dead?"

"It was you two who killed and robbed Oscar and he was a big fish back in Africa and now you two are going to pay with your lives." The African man said with a bloody smile. POW! POW! Victor put two bullets in the African's head silencing him forever.

"Damn!" Alex said. "What did you do that for? We could have gotten more information out of him."

"Fuck him" Victor replied. "We got all the information we need so let's go pay this Montana guy a visit." He said as he put a bullet in both of the prostitutes head before they exited the motel.

The Good Life

"Ahhhh yes daddy! Tear this pussy up!" Pink moaned as she buried her face down into the pillow while Jeezy put in work. He had Pink with her face down and her ass sticking up in the air. Jeezy stroked her as if he was trying to punish her. The louder she moaned the harder he pumped.

"Yes! Yes! Yes!" Pink screamed as she threw her ass back loving every stroke. She loved how Jeezy put it down in the bedroom. If it was one thing he knew how to do well, it was put it down in the bedroom. Jeezy quickly pulled out when he felt himself about to cum. Pink spun around quickly and sucked out every last drop.

"Damn!" Jeezy huffed laying on his back breathing heavily as he looked at his watch. "Damn I gotta get going."

"Where are you going baby" Pink asked? "You're not coming to the club with me tonight?"

"Nah, not tonight. I gotta drive up to the jail and go see Paige", he reminded her.

"Oh yeah that's right I forgot that was today" Pink said as she headed for the shower. "Have fun" she yelled over her shoulder.

Jeezy took a quick shower, got dressed, and was out the door in no time. Jeezy couldn't wait to see Paige face to face. Inside he was upset with himself for not going to see her yet, but he told himself from now on he would make a schedule for Paige. Jeezy could only imagine what she was going through in there. If it wasn't for her he don't know where he would be at right now. Jeezy was too busy trying to get everything set up for when Paige was released that he hadn't managed to visit her yet, but he made sure he sent her money every week and he always sent her monthly packages of food. Paige was allowed 35lbs of food a month and Jeezy always made sure she had more than enough. Jeezy pulled up to the federal facility and looked at his iPhone that read 11:24am. After getting searched and processed, he was finally allowed inside. The clock on visiting room wall read 12:35pm. Jeezy sat in the visiting room waiting for Paige to come out from the back. He walked over to the vending machine and got a cheeseburger, a chicken sandwich, and a Sprite. He knew it was the closest thing to real food that she could have until she was released. He walked over to the microwave and patiently waited for Paige's food to warm up. As Jeezy stood over by the microwave he looked at all the other women who had visitors. They all looked broke down and rough with the exception of a few. He felt sorry for all the women who were locked behind bars and away from their families. Twenty minutes later Paige finally came out from the back.

Jeezy smiled from ear to ear when he saw his fiancé walk through the doors. She looked a little thinner than the last time he had seen her, but he didn't care. He was just excited to see her.

"Heeeeeey baby!" Paige sang happily as she melted in Jeezy's arms hugging him tightly.

"I missed you so much" Jeezy said as he and Paige kissed sloppily getting nasty stares from all the C.O.'s. Once the two finished kissing Jeezy noticed a little bruise under Paige's eye.

"Fuck happened to your eye?" Jeezy asked instantly getting upset. "Nothing" Paige answered quickly as she sat down. " I'm fine. How have you been?" She tried to change the subject.

"Well that bruise, under your eye don't look like nothing" Jeezy pointed out. "Have these bitches in here have been bothering you?"

"I'm fine baby." Paige said struggling to fight back the tears. Inside she wanted to tell Jeezy the truth, but she didn't want him to be on the outside worrying about her. Paige knew what she had signed up for when she decided to take the charge.

"Don't bullshit me!" Jeezy said in a strong whisper looking Paige in her eyes. Paige could no longer fight back the tears as she broke down. "Baby I hate it here! I want to come home!"

"I know baby." Jeezy said feeling bad inside. He knew if it wasn't for him that she wouldn't even be in the situation that she was in.

"You don't have that much longer to go."

"These bitches in here are so mean and nasty." Paige sobbed. "It's inhumane in here."

"Is me sending you all the name brand shit you like getting you in trouble" Jeezy asked? He remembered when he was locked up how other inmates would get jealous because Paige was sending him all the name brand snacks that other inmates couldn't get.

"I'm just ready to come home." "How's everything going on the outside" she asked?

"Ahead of schedule" Jeezy told her. "Everything is looking real good baby and you know I'mma hold you down."
Just hearing that made Paige feel good inside. She knew Jeezy had her back, but seeing him face to face and just being able to touch him made her feel even better. Sitting in the visiting room with Jeezy was Paige's way to escape from the hell hole she was in. She didn't care if it was only for a few hours. It was better than nothing.

"Stay strong baby." "In 14 months you'll be back home" Jeezy told her. "I need you to be a soldier and thug this shit out."

"I am baby" Paige said forcing a smile on her face. "Can you please come visit me more?"

"Yes baby I got you. I just had to set everything up. Now that everything is all set up, I'll be up here to see you every week" Jeezy promised her.

"I know I speak to you every night, but I really need to see you more often."

"I got you baby" Jeezy promised her.

When Jeezy pulled out of the federal facility he felt good inside. He needed to see Paige just as much as she needed to see him. Jeezy felt bad that Paige was having problems inside because of the things he was sending her. He wanted her to have the things she needed, but at the same time he didn't want her getting her face pounded in over it either. Jeezy told himself that Paige would be out soon to make himself feel better. He knew she was going to have to hold it down for the time being while he took care of business on the outside. The rain came down hard as Jeezy made his way back towards the city.

***

Back at the strip club Pink bounced her ass to the sound of Yo Gotti bumping through the speakers. She had made a killing with the Ecstasy pills tonight in the club. Not to mention one of her regulars named Tyrone had been spending money with her all night. Pink didn't know where or how Tyrone got his money, but as long as he was spending it on her she could care less. She shook her ass in Tyrone's face for hours until he was finally out of money. Once Pink realized that the john was out of money she quickly headed over to the next john. You break one and go straight to the next one Pink thought as she scooped up all of her dollars from off the floor.

"Where are you going baby?" Tyrone asked grabbing Pink by her forearm a little more roughly then he had planned.

"You gotta pay to play baby!" Pink smiled as she jerked her arm away.

"So you just gone take all my money and head over to the next nigga?" Tyrone huffed. He had spent all of his money on her in hopes that maybe Pink would throw him some pussy to show her thanks. Tyrone had been coming to the same strip club for the past two weeks spending all of his money on Pink and tonight it was going to pay off whether Pink liked it or not he thought as he watched her and her fat ass strut off.

Pink quickly headed to the back and placed her money in her locker as she took a five minute break. Her thighs and calves were hurting from dancing all night. As Pink sat resting she thought about Jeezy. It felt weird that he wasn't at the club with her tonight, but she knew he had to go up to the jail to see Paige. Pink didn't like it, but she knew what the deal was from the jump. The problem was Pink had fell in love with Jeezy and that wasn't how things were supposed to go. Pink and Jeezy were just supposed to be business partners, nothing more and nothing less. The more time Pink started spending with Jeezy the more she started feeling him and eventually fell in love with him. Now that the two were living together it was a wrap in Pink's mind. Jeezy was her man and nobody was going to stop or come between that, point blank, period!

When her five minute break was over Pink put her stilettos back on and headed back out into the crowded club. She quickly found a spot on the pole and worked the pole for the rest of the night.

After an hour of shaking her ass and sliding down the pole Pink decided she was going to call it an early night and get home to her man. She missed Jeezy and wanted to surprise him by coming home early.

Pink quickly changed out of her stripper outfit and threw on a pair of Good2Go leggings, a tight fitting shirt, some flats, and was on her way out the door. As Pink strolled through the parking lot she heard some footsteps coming from behind her at a fast pace.

When Pink turned around she was quickly clothes lined down to the ground. Her body hit the ground like a sack of potatoes being dropped from a second floor window. Pink looked up and saw Tyrone standing over her.

"Bitch I done spent all my damn money on you and you think you just gone leave without giving me anything?" Tyrone snarled as he reached down and snatched Pink's pocketbook. He kicked Pink in her ribs as he continued to try and intimidate her with his ice grill.

"You got the money!" Pink yelled, "Now get the fuck outta here!" She could taste blood from her lip and her forearm was stinging badly.

Tyrone licked his lips taking a step forward. "You know what I want" he said as he snatched Pink's shirt right off her back.

Immediately Pink started kicking and screaming at the top of her lungs. Tyrone wanted to rape Pink right there in the parking lot, but she was screaming too loud drawing too much attention so instead he spun on his heels and took off running.

"Punk, Motherfucker!" Pink yelled as she stood to her feet and picked her car keys up from off the ground. When she had been clothes lined the strap on one of her shoes broke so Pink strolled through the rest of the parking lot bare foot. She hopped in her Audi and jetted out of the parking lot leaving the smell of burnt rubber in the air. Pink couldn't wait to get home and tell Jeezy what had happened. She knew when Jeezy caught up with Tyrone it wasn't going to be pretty.

***

Jeezy sat on the couch eating some Popeye's chicken and sipping on some vodka as the sound of Lil Wayne hummed at a medium volume through the speakers. Visiting with Paige had made his day. Jeezy's smile quickly turned into a frown when he saw Pink walk through the door bare foot with a busted lip.

"What the fuck happened to you?" Jeezy stood to his feet examining Pink from head to toe.

"I got robbed!" She cried as she slid in Jeezy's arms.

"Who robbed you?"

"One of my regular customers; some clown named Tyrone" Pink told him.

"Don't worry about it baby" Jeezy said stroking Pink's hair. "I'll take care of it." Inside Jeezy was furious. He wanted Tyrone dead for putting his hands on Pink. He didn't even care that he had robbed her. He knew his feeling for Pink shouldn't have been so strong, but he couldn't help it. He was now in too deep.

Hunting Season

Four men sat around the table playing cards. This was something that they did every Sunday. Each of the men worked for Montana. Neither of them liked or even enjoyed working for Montana, but what Montana was paying them was better than nothing. The men gambled every Sunday in the same run down one bedroom apartment in hopes to come up off the other.

Outside the front door Alex and Victor exited out of the staircase and headed straight to the gambling spot Alex swiftly whipped out his shotgun and blew the front door open. BOOM! He stepped inside the apartment and the first man to stand to his feet caught a blast to the chest. The other men sat at the table and watched as their partner skidded across the floor until his body crashed into a closet door from the impact of the Mossberg pump. Alex then quickly aimed his shotgun at the next man in line and pulled the trigger blowing the man's face completely off. His headless body jerked uncontrollably before sliding out of the chair and on to the floor.

"We're looking for Montana" Victor said as he stepped inside the apartment and pressed one of his .45's to the forehead of one of the men. Just as the man got ready to answer Victor pulled the trigger feeling like the man was taking too long for his liking. He watched as the man's body slithered out of the chair. Victor then quickly made it over to the last man standing. "Where's Montana?"

"Please man, don't kill me!" The man begged covering his head with his arms as if that was going to block a bullet. CLICK, CLACK! The sound of Alex pumping another round into the chamber of his shotgun caused the man to flinch.

"Alright! Alright! Alright!" The man said throwing his hands up in surrender. "Give me a pen and paper."

Victor smiled as he tossed a pen, at the man's face followed by a crumbled up napkin. "You got ten seconds."

The man handed Victor back the napkin with a scared look on his face. "You can catch Montana there every Friday."

Victor took the napkin and put a bullet right between the man's eyes silencing him forever. He looked down at the napkin and stuffed it down in his pocket as he and his brother made their exit.

No Turning Back

Paige sat on her bunk enjoying some bootleg Oreo cookies. After Roxy and Shawn had robbed her of all of her belongings, Paige used some of the money that Jeezy had sent her and purchased a few things from commissary. It wasn't as good as the things that Jeezy had brought her, but she would just have to make due until next month when she was allowed another 35lbs of food.

Paige couldn't stand all the other inmates or the fact that someone else told her when to eat and sleep and she most definitely couldn't stand how nasty the C.O.'s talked to the inmates as if they were trash.

As Paige sat on her bed she noticed Roxy and Shawn making their way over to her bunk. "What the fuck these bitches want now?" She mumbled under her breath.

"What's up, superstar?" Roxy said with an evil grin on her face while Shawn played the background with a stone look on her face.

"What yall want?" Paige said as if the two were an annoyance.

"My stomach is on the gate!" Roxy said rubbing her belly. "What you got over here for a bitch to eat?" She said as she began searching through Paige's locker.

Paige quickly hopped off of her bunk. She knew if she let the two dikes take her food again they would be taking her shit until her bid was over. She quickly walked over and shut her food locker door.

"Fuck is you doing?"
"I just told you a bitch is hungry!" Roxy repeated as she reached for the locker door again. Again Paige denied her access. In a quick motion Roxy pulled out a razor and faked like she was going to cut Paige. Paige quickly jumped back as Roxy and Shawn busted out laughing.

"Scary ass bitch!" Roxy laughed as she and Shawn emptied out Paige's food locker. "I'll catch you later superstar" Roxy said blowing Paige a kiss as she and Shawn made their way back over to the other side of the dorm.

Tears filled Paige's eyes as she hopped back up on her bunk and tried her hardest to fight them back. She couldn't understand why Roxy and all the other inmates targeted her.

"Fuck this shit!" Paige huffed as she wiped her face, hopped off her bunk, and headed towards the dayroom. "Enough is enough" she said to herself. Paige knew if she didn't put an end to this foolishness now than it would never stop. She entered the dayroom and noticed a few of the other inmates dancing to Trey Songz video "Bottoms Up" that played on the T.V. Screen. Paige spotted Rose right up in front of the TV. She quickly made her way through the hot women all lusting over Trey Songz and tapped Rose on her shoulder.
"Hey girl" Rose said giving Paige a friendly hug. "I was wondering when you were going to come out in the day room. You stay glued to that bunk!"

"Can I speak to you over in private for a second?" Paige said as the two walked out of ear shot of all the other women.

"What's on your mind?" Rose asked seriously once she saw the concerned look on Paige's face.
"I need a shank" Paige told her.

Rose smiled as she looked Paige up and down. She knew it would only be a matter of time before the innocent woman who stood before her snapped. "You sure you wanna do this?"

Paige nodded her head yes. If she didn't make a stand now those bitches would be taking her shit forever. Paige followed Rose back to her bunk.

"Watch my back" Rose said as she bent down, lifted the edge of her locker, and slid a plastic homemade shank from under her locker. "Here" she handed the shank to Paige. "If you get caught, you didn't get that from me."

Paige held the shank in her hand. Right then and there she knew it was no turning back. She was about to do something that she never in her life thought she would ever have to do; take someone's life.

"So what do I do now" Paige asked? "Just go up to her and stab her right now?"

"No! Unless you wanna stay in here for the rest of your life" Rose said seriously. "You wait and catch that bitch off guard. You strike when she least expects it. When she is showering or maybe when she is taking a shit."

"Okay" Paige said, but inside she was scared to death. She didn't want to hurt anybody, but when in Rome you gotta do what the Romans do.

"Don't worry I'll be with you the whole way and guide you through the whole thing" Rose told her.

"Is this the only option I have" Paige huffed?

"Yes!" Rose snapped. "You better toughen up and get with the fucking program." She paused. "What happens next time if you try to stick up for yourself and Roxy and the rest of them hoes stick a shank up in you; then what?"

Paige hated to admit it, but Rose was right. This was the only way. It was sad but, the truth was ignorant people only respect violence. For the rest of the day Paige and Rose kept a close watch on Roxy. Since Paige was out of food she didn't have to worry about Roxy harassing her. About two hours later Paige noticed Roxy rushing to the restroom carrying a role of tissue.

"Now's your chance" Rose said excitedly nudging Paige with her elbow. Paige swallowed hard as she stood to her feet. On the outside she looked fine, but on the inside she was a nervous wreck.

Rose quickly picked up Paige's nervousness. "Look, it's either now or never!" She said firmly.

"Fuck it" Paige said under her breath as she entered the restroom. She gripped the shank tightly as she stood outside the stall that Roxy occupied.

Rose stood by the entrance and signaled to Paige that the coast was clear.
Paige took a deep breath as she took a step forward and kicked open the stall door. Inside she saw Roxy sitting on the toilet with a mean look on her face.

"Bitch close this mufucking door before you be shitting your teeth" Roxy threatened.

Paige swiftly plunged the shank into Roxy and then twisted it. Roxy had a shocked look on her face as she tried to rise to her feet. Paige roughly pushed her back down as she plunged the shank in and out of Roxy's body thirteen more times before she exited the stall in a sprint.

Rose quickly grabbed Paige and pulled her over towards the sinks. "Don't run" she said in a harsh whisper as she took the shank from Paige's hand and rinsed it off. "Go sit in the day room and wait for me."

Paige quickly washed the blood from her hands and exited the restroom trying to look as normal as possible. Rose washed the blood off the shank and exited the restroom seconds later. As she headed back towards the bunks Rose wiped her prints clean then placed the shank under Roxy's pillow and kept it moving.

Back in the dayroom Paige sat in the corner with a nervous look on her face. She just knew that she and Rose were going to get caught. Paige felt a hand touch her shoulder and almost jumped out of her skin.

"Relax" Rose said in a warm tone. Seconds later several inmates ran towards the restroom when they heard someone scream.

"Oh my God" Paige said in a defeated tone.
"Pull yourself together!" Rose warned her as they both got up and headed towards the restroom along with the rest of the

inmates so thing didn't look suspicious. "No matter what happens; keep your mouth shut!"

Minutes later the dorm was flooded with C.O.'s wearing riot gear. Immediately every inmate was forced down to the floor as the C.O.'s conducted a search.

"Ah shit! What did I just do?" Paige thought to herself as she laid face down on the floor watching the C.O.'s tear the dorm up looking for the murder weapon. Each inmate was then order to stand to their feet and hold out their hands. The C.O.'s were looking for any cuts or bruises that may have indicated they had anything to do with the murder.

Paige watched nervously as the C.O.'s went down the line looking at each woman's hands. A few women were snatched out of the line because their hands had minor bruises on them. Paige took a deep breath as the C.O.'s stood in front of her.

"Hands!" The lady C.O. said coldly as she examined Paige's hands front and back. After about twenty seconds of looking over Paige's hands the C.O. moved on to the next woman in line. Paige closed her eyes and exhaled as she said a quick silent prayer. She looked over at Rose who was now getting her hands checked by a male C.O. A small thankful grin appeared on Paige's face when the male C.O. skipped past Rose.

"You bitches want to act like fucking animals" the captain announced. "Then that's how ya'll will be treated from now on until we find out who is responsible for this murder. This place is officially on lock down!" He said then made his exit.
As all the inmates headed back to their bunks Paige noticed a few chicks holding Shawn back. "Bitch I know it was you" she

yelled pointing at Paige. Paige ignored the ignorant woman and kept it moving towards her bunk.

"You better watch your back bitch!" Shawn threatened as she was escorted to her bunk. When Paige reached her bunk her bunky Big Momma sucked her teeth. "You're a dead woman walking."

"What you talking about?" Paige asked faking ignorance.

"Bitch don't play stupid" Big Momma huffed. "Everybody knows it was you that stabbed Roxy."

"I didn't stab anybody" Paige lied as she climbed up on her bunk.
Big Momma chuckled. "Yeah alright!"

Paige lay on her bed looking up at the ceiling. She wondered if Big Momma was telling the truth and did everyone really know that it was her who had killed Roxy? If they did know it was her; she didn't have to worry about nobody snitching because it was a no snitching no matter what rule in jail when it came to telling on another inmate. This meant Paige didn't have to worry about getting caught for the murder and spending the rest of her life jail for it. Instead now she had to worry about making it out of jail alive especially if all of Roxy's crew knew she was the one responsible for the death of their leader.

Don't Start No Shit

Jeezy woke up and noticed that he was in the king sized bed all alone. He quickly sat straight up and took a strong sniff. Whenever he woke up alone it was usually because Pink was in the kitchen making him breakfast; something she did every day since the two of them began living together. When Jeezy didn't smell anything cooking he quickly reached over and grabbed his 40 caliber from off the night stand and went to investigate. After searching the entire house Jeezy sat on the bar stool puzzled. Pink never left the house without notifying Jeezy. He picked up his iPhone and just as Jeezy was about to dial her number he heard keys jingling at the front door. Seconds later Pink walked through the front door in a white blouse, white dress pants, and a pair of three inch white pumps to match the bright smile on her face.

"Sorry baby I tried to make it back before you woke up" she confessed.

"Where were you" Jeezy asked? "I was about to start getting worried."

"It's a surprise" Pink smiled. "Close your eyes" she sang as she guided Jeezy towards the front door. "Surprise!" Pink said snatching the front door open.

Jeezy opened his eyes and saw an all black Range Rover sitting in the drive way sitting on black rims.

"You like it baby?" Pink asked excitedly.

"Yes baby!" "I was just thinking about copping a new ride" Jeezy said checking out all the features of the truck.

"Well I'm glad you like it, because my man will only be riding around in the best" Pink smiled.

Jeezy ignored that last comment. He knew Pink was beginning to become too attached to him, but it was no way he could turn down a brand new Range Rover. Ever since moving in with Pink, Jeezy had yet to go in his pocket for anything. Pink was a strong believer in taking good care of her man. No man of hers would ever have to cook, clean, or even lift a finger as long as she was alive.

"Want to take a ride with me for breakfast in your new ride" Pink asked?

"Give me twenty minutes to take a shower and get dressed" Jeezy said quickly disappearing in the house.

***

Later on that night Jeezy pulled up in front of the strip club and watched as Pink grabbed her duffle bag, kissed him on the lips, then headed in the club. Jeezy cruised through the parking lot until he finally found a spot. From how packed the parking lot was he knew that Pink was going to make a killing in the strip club tonight with the E pills. Inside the strip club was packed just like Jeezy expected it to be. He quickly made his way over to his usual table over in the cut and took a seat. Jeezy scanned the club twice hoping he saw Tyrone. He hadn't forgotten about what he did to Pink, while he was away visiting Paige. Jeezy knew he was going to run into him sooner or later and he couldn't wait.

As soon as Pink stepped foot in the locker room all of the other strippers were all over her in need of some E pills. She quickly distributed the pills and collected the cash. Pink changed into a cute stripper outfit and began making her rounds throughout the club. Time was money and she didn't plan on wasting neither.

Jeezy sat sipping on a drink when he noticed all the attention in the club sway towards the entrance. Seconds later Jeezy saw Montana and two of his bodyguards enter the club followed by Big Tone with six of his goons in tow. Immediately Jeezy knew tonight wasn't going to be an ordinary night. All he wanted to do was sit in the cut and get paid, but he quickly dismissed that thought when he saw Montana heading over in his direction.

"My main man Jeezy" Montana greeted. "What you doing up in here and why you sitting over here in the cut like this?"

"You know being all in the spot light has never been my thing" Jeezy replied as the two shook hands.

"I heard it's some bad bitches up in here." Montana smiled. Jeezy returned his smile, but inside he wanted to tell Montana to beat it. Jeezy had better things to do than engage in small talk with his former boss.

"I'mma get up with you before I leave" Montana said as him and his two bodyguards walked off. "You sit here in the cut all you want but I'm about to hop on one of these bitches."
Jeezy sipped on his drink as Big Tone walked past his table with a stone look on his face. The bad blood between the two men was visible. Even the bouncers noticed it. Jeezy shook

his head at how ignorant Big Tone was as he finished up his drink.

"When you gone let me kill that faggot?" Big Tone said looking over at Montana. "That nigga is up to something. I just don't know what yet."

Montana laughed. "All these beautiful ladies up in here and you're worried about little ole Jeezy?" He laughed some more. "I think you got more things that deserve your attention than him."

"I know, but I just don't like that nigga for some reason." Big Tone huffed.

"We in the drug business, not the beef business" Montana reminded him. Montana knew the two men didn't like each other, but he just didn't know exactly why nor did he care. As long as they weren't messing with his money he could care less.

Jeezy helped himself to another drink as Fabulous' song "You Be Killin Em" came blaring through the speakers. He looked up and saw Pink on the stage seductively dancing on the pole. She held the entire club's attention when she dropped down into a full split as she continued to pop each one of her ass cheeks simultaneously getting cheers from all of the howling men and women. Jeezy sat back with a grin on his face. He felt good to know that all the men in the strip club wanted his woman.

Pink worked the stage and pole like an expert until the song finally went off. As she swept up all of her money from off the stage floor she felt a strong hand grab her wrist. She looked up and saw Big Tone undressing her with his eyes.

"What's up wit it?" Big Tone said sounding like the ignorant fool that he was.

"What's up with what?" Pink sucked her teeth yanking her wrist away from his grip with a disgusted look on her face.

"How much is it going to cost for some of that sweet pussy" Big Tone said flashing a huge knot of money. He believed that all strippers were high priced prostitutes.

"You couldn't afford it!" Pink countered as she continued to scoop up her singles. She hated when stupid drunk men came into the strip club just looking to belittle women.

"Bitch you know you want all this" Big Tone said as if he was God's gift to women. His arm shot out and pulled Pink close to him as he began rubbing all over her horse ass.

"Get your filthy hands off of me!" Pink raised her voice causing a scene. Once Pink decided to raise her voice Big Tone became even more aggressive. Just as Big Tone was about to slip one of Pink's nipples in his mouth, he felt somebody forcefully push him from behind. When Big Tone turned around he saw Jeezy standing there.

"Yo my man" Jeezy began. "Fall back or either get pushed back!"
Big Tone was about to smack Jeezy's head off of his shoulders until two bouncers stepped in between the two.

"Is there a problem over here?" One of the bouncers asked looking over at Pink.

"No" Pink answered quickly as she snatched up her money and headed back to the dressing room.

"You good" the bouncer said looking at Big Tone. "Yeah, I'm straighter than Indian hair" he joked assuring the bouncer that he was cool. Once the bouncer walked off Big Tone lunged towards Jeezy tackling him on to the stage causing a loud booming sound to erupt. This is what the two had been waiting for. Now it wasn't nothing but space and opportunity in between them. The two men went at it like caged animals going blow for blow; each man trying to drop the other with one punch. Seconds later several bouncers tackled both men off the stage.

Pink stood in the dressing room putting away her money when she heard a loud commotion coming from near the stage. She quickly ran back out to the stage in her four inch heels. When she reached the stage she saw two bouncers separating Jeezy and Big Tone. Pink removed one of her heels and started banging Big Tone in the back of his head like she was trying to bang a nail into a wall until a bouncer came over and restrained her.

"Cock blocking mufucka!" Big Tone yelled as he was roughly escorted out of the club.

"You alright baby?" Pink asked checking to see if Jeezy was okay. She knew once that clown had grabbed her all hell was going to break loose.

"I'm good baby" Jeezy said fixing his clothes. Now he had to figure out how he was going to get to his car in one piece and retrieve his gun without getting shot. In the midst of the scuffle Montana and his two bodyguards slipped out the back door unnoticed.

When Jeezy and Pink stepped outside they saw Big Tone and his crew arguing with the police.

"Come on baby" Jeezy said as he and Pink made a bee line straight for the Range Rover. Once inside Jeezy grabbed his 40 caliber from under his seat and placed it on his lap.

"No baby!" Pink grabbed his arm gently. "Let it go" she said sincerely looking in Jeezy's eyes. Jeezy wasn't the one for walking away from a fight, but he knew what Pink was saying was right. There was a time and place for everything and now wasn't the time nor the place.

"Thanks baby!" Pink smiled as Jeezy pulled out of the parking lot. As Jeezy drove he felt Pink unzipping his pants and seconds later he felt her warm mouth all over his dick. Pink sloppily sucked on Jeezy's dick as her head bobbed up and down at a fast pace. Jeezy did his best to remain focused on the road as Pink forced him to explode in her mouth. When Jeezy pulled up in the driveway he and Pink kissed all the way inside the house as they prepared for round two.

***

Back at the strip club, Alex and Victor sat camped out in a low key stolen car watching the entire scene play out. What they noticed was that everybody had exited the club except for Montana.

"Where is this fucker" Victor asked in an angry tone. He woke up in a bad mood and couldn't wait to take his anger out on someone else.

"I don't know" Alex answered in a calm tone, "but I know who does" he said nodding his head towards Big Tone.

"Bitch ass nigga" Big Tone huffed as he hopped in his Escalade leaving the scene. If it was one thing Big Tone couldn't stand was a cock blocker and in his eyes that's just what Jeezy was; a punk ass cock blocker. He was already planning on what he was going to do to Jeezy the next time the two ran into each other. When he pulled into his driveway Drake's song "I'm On One" bumped through the Escalade's speakers. Big Tone killed the engine and hopped out. Still pissed off from what happened at the strip club Big Tone didn't know someone was creeping up behind him until he heard the paralyzing sound of a round being cocked into the chamber of a shotgun.

"Don't do it to yourself big man" Alex warned shoving the Mossberg pump into Big Tone's spine as he snatched his keys and roughly forced Big Tone inside the house tossing him down on the floor like he was trash.

"I'm looking for Montana! Where can I find him?"

"Go suck a dick" Big Tone huffed waving the two gunmen off. Snitching was something that he would never do. "Fuck!" "Am I supposed to be scared because you two pussies are waving guns around" he said trying to buy himself some time. Just by looking at the two men from the jump he knew he was being held at gun point by the Gambino Brothers which meant they were there for a reason.

Alex was about to respond until he heard what sounded like a baby crying coming from upstairs. "Who else is in the house?"

"My wife and my eight month old son," Big Tone announced with a worried look on his face. "Please don't hurt them."

Alex ignored his plea. "Where's Montana" he asked again? When Big Tone didn't answer Alex turned to Victor and gave him a go ahead nod.

Big Tone watched as Victor flew up the steps taking them two at a time. "Hey" he yelled! "Where's he going? Come back!"
Seconds later there were screams and the sound of furniture moving coming from upstairs. Alex grinned as he looked down at Big Tone.

"Okay I'll tell you where Montana is; just please make your brother stop" Big Tone screamed. He thought about trying to make a move, but he had heard rumors and stories about how nice Alex Gambino was with a shotgun and decided against it. Minutes later Victor came down the steps with blood all over his face and hands. In one of his hands he held a bloody hunting knife.
"What did you do? You sick bastard!" Big Tone yelled.

"That damn baby wouldn't shut up so I put him to sleep" Victor said flashing a grin as he cleaned off his knife.

"Address" Alex said in a calm tone. Once Big Tone gave up Montana's address Alex blasted him in the chest twice leaving him for dead in his own living room.

I Need You

Pink moaned loudly as Jeezy had her standing up bent over the couch deep stroking her. Lately Pink had been turning into a nympho requesting and begging for sex every day. Sometimes even two and three times a day. Jeezy did his best to quench Pink's sexual appetite, but he wasn't a machine.

Jeezy grabbed a hand full of Pink's hair and aggressively pulled her head back forcing her to look up at him while he pounded away at her insides. "Do this dick feel good?"

"Yes baby! Yes!" Pink moaned loving every stroke.

"Tell me you love this dick" Jeezy demanded as he pumped even harder.

"Oooh I love this dick! I love this dick! Ahhhh baby I love this dick!" Pink repeated loudly as Jeezy quickly spun her around and snatched off his condom. Immediately Pink threw Jeezy's dick in her mouth and sucked on it like it was the last dick she was ever going to see until Jeezy released in her mouth.

"Oh shit" Jeezy huffed as he quickly went and hopped in the shower. Seconds later Jeezy felt a pair of hands grab his waist from behind.

"That dick was the best" Pink grinned.

"So glad you enjoyed it" Jeezy said cleaning himself off in a rush.

"Where are you rushing off to" Pink asked suspiciously. Jeezy looked at her like she was crazy. "You know I gotta go see Paige today."

"Damn I forgot all about that" Pink lied. Really she was tired of him going up to the jail to see Paige. She was hoping that once she started taking care of Jeezy that maybe he would forget all about his jail bitch. "Can't you just spend the day with me and go see her tomorrow? For me pleeeeease?" She whined.

"No can do" Jeezy replied quickly as he stepped out of the shower leaving Pink standing in the shower alone. "I have to go see her. She needs my support."

"But I need your support too baby" Pink whined stepping out of the shower dripping wet. "Since I'm a big part in your life now, you going to have to make time for the both of us."

"I see you every day and I see her once a week" Jeezy reminded her. "Don't start! You know I have to go."

"Fine!" Pink said with an attitude as she stomped out of the bathroom. Jeezy shook his head when he heard the bedroom door slam. Pink was becoming too attached to him and now was the time to start detaching himself from her especially since Paige would be getting released eight months from today. Jeezy quickly got dressed and was out the door.

As he cruised down the highway his mind began thinking of ways he could let Pink go easily because he knew once Paige got out there was no way she was going to put up with that shit. Jeezy wondered how Pink would take it once he informed her that he could no longer deal with her. Pink was a good woman. If he wasn't with Paige then he would definitely stay with Pink, but that wasn't the situation. Jeezy was loyal to Paige so he had eight months to figure out how he was going to cut Pink loose.

Jeezy went through the visiting process and was finally allowed in the visiting room. He went and grabbed all the snacks he knew that Paige liked and had them waiting at the table for her. Ten minutes later Paige walked out from the back. From where Jeezy was sitting Paige had been putting on weight in all the right places.

Paige smiled as she melted in Jeezy's arms and tried to squeeze the life out of him. "I missed you so much" she whispered in his ear.

"I missed you too baby" Jeezy replied as he sat down. As soon as Jeezy looked in Paige's eyes he could tell that something was wrong. "What's wrong baby?"

"Nothing" Paige replied as tears slowly rolled down her cheeks.
"Talk to me baby" Jeezy said softly as he held on to her hands. He could always tell when something was bothering her just by looking in her eyes.

"This place has really changed me" Paige cried. "I'm not the same person that I was before I came in here."

Immediately Jeezy thought she meant that somebody had took his pussy while she was on the inside. "Tell me what happened baby and be honest."

Paige cried a little bit more before she spoke in a light whisper. "I killed a woman."

Jeezy took a second to digest what Paige had just told him. He knew that no matter what happened; murdering someone was something that would stick with Paige forever mentally as well as physically.

"I had no choice" Paige told him. "If I didn't do it eventually..."

"It's okay baby you don't have to explain" Jeezy said cutting her off. "You did what you had to do. All I ask is that you protect yourself by any means necessary."

"Now the bitch home girls all got it out for me" Paige said.

"We only got eight months left to go" Jeezy said as he heard the C.O. announce that visiting hours were over. "Eight months" he repeated.

"I'll survive" Paige said forcing a fake smile on her face so Jeezy wouldn't be worried about her.

"I know you will baby" Jeezy said as he watched the C.O. escort Paige into the back.

Once in the back Paige was forced to strip down butt naked as she was thoroughly searched by a female C.O. When that was over she was allowed back to her dorm. A visit from Jeezy was just what Paige needed. He some how always seemed to ease her mind and make things seem as if they were going to be okay.

When Paige made it back to her bunk she noticed that her bunky wasn't around so she quickly hopped up on her bunk and threw her head phones on. Right now she just needed to listen to some music and zone out. Paige popped in her Neyo cassette tape and closed her eyes as the soft sound of Neyo filled her ears. For once since she'd been in jail, Paige was actually having a good day. Her good day quickly came to an end when she felt some one shaking her bed. When Paige opened her eyes and looked up she saw a rough looking chick standing in her cube. She didn't know the chick, but had seen her hanging around Roxy a few times.

"Yo I need to borrow your head phones for a second" the chick said scratching her head.

"What" Paige said looking at the rough chick like she was insane.
"I'm bored as hell right now so I need to borrow your head phones for a few. So what's up?" The chick said as if Paige was getting on her nerves.

"Don't you see me using them right now" Paige said.
"Bitch you trying to get fly over some head phones" the chick said rolling up her sleeves like she was ready to get busy. "You are fucking with the wrong one!" She said stepping back throwing up her hands making a scene.

"All this over some head phones though" Paige thought as she removed her head phones, slid them under her pillow, then hopped off the top bunk. Just as the two was about to get it on one of the cool male C.O's. interfered. "What the hell is going on over here?" He asked.

"I need five minutes with this bitch" the chick said to the C.O. waiting for his approval. The C.O. looked over at Paige and asked her did she want five minutes with the rough looking chick. Every time he'd seen Paige she was mostly to herself, minding her business. He wondered why someone like her would want to have a fight with the rougher looking chicks.

"Yeah I want five minutes" Paige stated as she removed her button up shirt exposing her sports bra. Paige quick ran up on the rough chick and swung on her catching her off guard. Paige went toe to toe with the chick until the chick decided to grab her. She flung Paige down to the floor like a rag doll as she began raining down punches on her. Paige balled up trying to block as many of the blows as possible. As she lay with her back on the floor, she prayed that the C.O. would break up the fight, but instead he was on the sideline cheering with the rest of the inmates. The rough chick landed blow after blow on Paige until Rose came out of nowhere and smacked the rough looking chick in the back of the head with a thick five hundred page hard back dictionary knocking her out cold. Paige quickly shot to her feet and began stomping the chicks face into the floor. She made animal noises as she stomped until the C.O. finally snatched her off the chick.

"That's enough!" The C.O. yelled in Paige's face to get her attention. She looked as if she was possessed at the moment.

"Alright! Alright! The shows over!" He announced as he made the rest of the inmates go on about their business. "There's nothing else to see here!"

"Good looking I appreciate that" Paige said walking up to Rose. "I done had enough of this shit" she admitted. "Once I leave this shit hole in eight months I ain't ever coming back!"

"Don't mention it" Rose smiled. "I know you would have done it for me."

"Bitch this shit ain't over with. I'mma see you" Shawn said as she walked past breaking up the two's conversation. All

Paige could do was shake her head. She knew that this harassment wasn't going to be over with until she and Shawn got it on. The tension in the air was so thick you could cut it with a knife. The question wasn't where they would bump into each other, but when.

Doing the Right Thing

Jeezy's Range Rover pulled into his driveway then shortly after the engine was shut off. Jeezy slowly slid out of the driver seat. Tonight was the night he decided to tell Pink that they were going to have to slow down a bit. He'd been thinking about how he was going to deliver the message to her, easy and gently as possible.

Jeezy stuck his key in the door and immediately the door snatched open, causing him to jump back a bit.

Pink stood at the door wearing some sexy white lingerie. She grabbed Jeezy's hand and led him inside. As Jeezy stepped through the house he noticed that there were candles lit up all around the house along with rose pedals sprinkled all throughout the house.

"What's all this for?" Jeezy asked looking around.

"I just want you to know that I'm so sorry for how I acted before you left" Pink apologized. "Paige was around before me and as much as I hate sharing you, I knew what I was getting into from the beginning and I'm sorry."

"It's cool" Jeezy said, "but for real though I can't have you acting like that. Paige will be home soon and if you continue to act like this then I'mma have to cut you loose."

"Nigga please" Pink laughed. "Ain't no getting rid of me that easy" she laughed again, but she was dead serious. Just as Jeezy was about to say something else Pink quickly hushed him as she roughly shoved him down on the couch. "I been waiting for you to get home all day so you could taste this good pussy" she said raising one leg up on the couch. Jeezy licked his lips as he looked at Pink's freshly waxed pussy. Just the site of it got Jeezy's dick to stand at attention. Pink seductively climbed up on the couch standing over Jeezy. "Tell me how bad you wanna eat this pussy" she whispered, turning around making both of her ass cheeks vibrate in his face. Jeezy couldn't take it no more as he aggressively pulled Pink's ass down into his face. Pink squatted down backwards on Jeezy's face. "Ahhhhh! Yes!" Pink moaned gyrating her ass further down into Jeezy's face. For the rest of the night the two went at it like newlyweds.

Uninvited Guest

Montana lay in his bed watching a porno while he waited for his lady friend to get out of the shower. He had planned on giving the woman a fucking she would never forget. Just as Montana heard the shower water cut off, he heard several back to back thunderous gunshots coming from downstairs.

"Shit!" Montana cursed as he hopped up off his bed and grabbed his 9mm from off the night stand.

"What the fuck was that" his lady friend asked sticking her head out the bathroom door. Montana ignored her as he exited the bedroom and looked down over the balcony. Immediately he knew he was fucked when he saw one of the Gambino Brothers downstairs.

Alex aimed his shotgun up at Montana. "Drop that gun!" He ordered with a smile on his face.

"What do y'all want" Montana countered?

"Don't make me ask you again" Alex repeated slowly stepping up the stairs. Finally Montana dropped his gun down to the floor.
"Why do you want me and my brother dead" Alex asked kicking Montana's gun out of reach.

"Let me explain" Montana said with his palms up. "I'm in business with some very important men and they thought that you and your brother had something to do with one of their associates being killed and robbed. "So they put a bounty on your head" he told him. "but I can get them to take the bounty off you and your brother's head and I'm also going to offer you two a job. If y'all are interested."

"A job doing what" Victor asked finally making his way up the steps.

"Doing what you two do best" Montana smiled. "Me and my people can line up all the heavy weights and all ya'll would have to do is rob them blind."

"What's your cut?" Alex asked.

"Twenty five percent of everything yall take" Montana replied.
"How we know this shit is real?" Victor asked skeptically.
"How we know you won't set us up or turn us in to the police?"

"The last thing you and your brother would have to worry about is the police" Montana assured him. "Like I told you my associates are very powerful men and can make any charge go away; especially if you guys are doing good business."

"This sounds too good to be true." Alex cocked a round into the chamber of his shotgun. "What's the catch?" Ever since he was a kid, the only person he ever trusted was his brother Victor and vice versa. Something about the offer Montana was presenting seemed too good to be true.

"You and your brother do one job. If ya'll don't like it then ya'll can walk." "No strings attached" Montana promised.

"Give us a few days to think about it" Victor said, "but in the mean time you are going to have to pay if you wanna keep your life."

Montana smiled. "How much?"

"$200,000" Victor returned Montana's smile. "Nothing personal just business."

The Gambino Brothers followed Montana in the master bedroom over to his safe. Victor wanted to rob Montana and kill him on the spot, but his brother Alex gave him a silent signal to chill. Unlike Victor, Alex was looking at the big picture.

Montana returned from his safe and handed a bag filled with $200,000 to Victor. "There's plenty more where that came from" he said with a smile.

"We'll be in touch" Alex said as he and Victor exited the bedroom and headed for the door.

"Hey!" Montana called after the two brothers causing them to stop dead in their tracks. "How do I get in touch with you two?"

"You don't" Alex replied. "We'll get in touch with you" he said, and then the two brothers were gone.

The Inevitable

Paige walked down the hallway half listening to what Rose was joking about. Her mind was on a much more serious matter. The word going around the prison was, today was the day that Paige was going to get what was coming to her. All of Roxy's associates still couldn't get over what Paige had done to their leader. Even though they didn't have any proof all fingers still pointed in Paige's direction. Even if Paige wasn't the one responsible for Roxy's murder she was the one who had been chosen to take the blame whether she liked it or not.

In Paige's pocket rested a shank. This was the same shank she had used to kill Roxy. Paige didn't want any trouble, but at the same time she had to protect herself by any means. Paige and Rose stepped foot in the mess hall and immediately the voice and chatter from all the other inmates attacked their ears. "Relax" Rose said sensing her friend's nervousness. "Ain't nobody dumb enough to pull a stunt in the mess hall. They will charge you as starting a riot for that" she said confidently.

"I hope you're right" Paige replied. She hoped that what Rose was saying was true, but in her heart she could feel the heat in the air. All she had to do was survive for the next six months and then she would be a free woman. "All you have to do is survive." She told herself over and over as she grabbed a tray and went down the food line. The women who served her gave her nasty looks as she went down the line. Paige ignored the looks and kept it moving. She didn't have time to worry about the other inmates. She had much more important shit to be worried about like staying alive. Paige followed behind Rose as the two searched for a place to sit. Paige noticed all the weird looks that the other inmates were giving her. She mentally began to prepare herself for the worst. As Rose headed over to an available seat Shawn hopped up out of her seat and shoved a knife in Rose several times until her body collapsed down to the floor. Other inmates roared out of excitement when they saw the murder committed right before their eyes.

Shawn didn't say a word instead she headed straight for Paige next. Paige quickly tossed her tray into Shawn's face, giving her time to pull her shank out of her pocket.

"Yeah bitch let's go!" Shawn growled as she and Paige stood only a few feet away from each other. Shawn swung her knife at Paige's throat. Paige quickly jumped back as she sliced Shawn's arm in the process. Shawn took another swipe at Paige, but came up short again. Paige took a few steps back and looked around wondering where all the C.O.'s were.

Tired of the cat and mouse game Shawn charged towards Paige. Paige tried to side step her, but Shawn's hands were too quick. She felt the sharp knife plunge into her stomach and thought she was going to die right there on the spot. Paige roughly pushed Shawn off of her slicing her across her face at the same time. Shawn dropped her knife when she felt warm blood trickling down her face. Paige also dropped her shank so she could use two hands to hold the wound on her stomach.
When Shawn realized her face had been cut she charged Paige running full speed tackling her on top of a table where she rained punch after punch down on Paige's unexposed face until finally several C.O.'s came and tackled Shawn off of Paige. When the C.O.'s arrived Paige was barely conscious. Still they

hand cuffed both women and rushed them to the nurse's office, and then straight to the hospital.

Six Months Later

Jeezy cut the shower water off and just stood in the shower for a second trying to gather his thoughts together. Today was the day he had to break the news to Pink that he could no longer deal with her on an intimate level. He'd been trying to tell her for the past six months, but for some reason it never happened. Jeezy took a deep breath as he stepped out of the bathroom to handle his business. When he stepped foot in the room Pink was right there waiting for him with his iPhone in her hand.

"Who are all these bitches in your phone" Pink asked with a crazy look in her eyes.

"None of your business" Jeezy barked snatching his phone from her hands. "Fuck is you all up in my shit for anyway?"

"Because I knew your ass was up to something. I just didn't have any proof, but now I do so explain" she said with her arms folded across her chest.

Jeezy shook his head in disgust as he looked Pink up and down. The sad part of the whole thing was he really wasn't fooling around with anyone. Those women were just a few women he flirted with every now, and then. "Ain't nothing to explain!" He waved Pink off as he began to get dressed.

"Oh so you ain't got shit to say now cause your ass is busted right" Pink huffed. "I swear can't shit a man do to surprise me. I have done, seen, and heard it all."

"You right" Jeezy said over his shoulder as he continued to get dressed.

"So while I'm out shaking my ass to get us both paid, this is what you do in your spare time. You are out here fucking these raggedy ass bitches!"

"You right" Jeezy said sarcastically only getting Pink madder then she already was.

"That's your problem you think everything is a fucking joke" Pink continued her rant. "It's cool though."
"You right!"

Pink quickly hopped up off the bed, getting up in Jeezy's face. "Say you right again! Please say it again!"

"Yo back up" Jeezy said pushing her a few feet back with his hand.
"Ain't no back up nothing!" Pink yelled smacking Jeezy's hand off of her chest. "Our whole relationship is one big joke to you right? Be honest!"

"Listen," Jeezy said seriously. "We never had a relationship. The only relationship we have, excuse me had was a business relationship!"

"Ooooooh okay now cause your little girlfriend is getting out of jail in two weeks you don't need me no more" Pink said shaking her head up and down pacing back and forth in the bedroom. She had a feeling that Jeezy was going to try to kick her to the curb when Paige was released from jail.

"Listen baby you are a wonderful and beautiful woman." He paused, "but I told you from day one that I was engaged and that my fiancé was locked up."

"So what about our business at the club?"

"It's all yours" Jeezy told her. "I'll introduce you to my E pill connect so you'll be straight."

"You a grimy ass nigga" Pink said as tears rolled down her cheeks. "So now because Paige is getting out of jail you just gonna leave a bitch for dead like that? I thought you was better than that!"

Jeezy knew Pink was going to try to make him feel bad about his decision. He also knew it wasn't going to be easy. Inside he did feel bad about having to let her go, but at the end of the day it was the best move. "I would love to continue to do business with you, but I don't think it would work."

"Whatever!" Pink flicked her hand in a dismissive manner. "Go be with your queen, cause obviously she's more precious than gold" she said laughing at her own joke. "You want the bitch, then go be with her. Just know once you walk out that door ain't no coming back!"

"You right" Jeezy replied as he grabbed the four duffle bags of money that he had been saving up and his 40 caliber and was out the door.

"I need a real man anyway!" Pink yelled out the front door at Jeezy's departing back. "Not some little boy who runs every time his bitch tells him too!" "Pussy!" she yelled and then slammed the door. Once the door shut Pink placed her back to the door, slid down to the floor, and cried her eyes out. The one man that had treated her like a queen and never judged her for what she did for a living had just walked out of her front door and took her heart with him.

Money Talks

Alex parked the Maximum across the street from the house of some brothers from Alabama who were supposed to be making some major chips. Montana had sent the Gambino Brothers out to Alabama to teach the brothers a lesson. He had offered them a nice price on the coke, but when they turned the offer down that didn't sit too well with Montana. Now the Gambino Brothers were in Alabama to send a message.

"This the crib right here" Victor asked with a frown on his face from the passenger seat. He hated being in the country. Things seemed to just move too slowly for him.

"Yeah that's it" Alex replied as he loaded up his Mossberg before they hopped out the vehicle and headed towards the front door.

Steve sat at the kitchen table talking to his baby's mother Lisa while his younger brother Anthony sat in the living room playing play station with a few of his homeboys. Steve sat at the kitchen table making plans with Lisa on whether or not he should invest some of his money in a laundry mat business. Lisa jumped when the front door came busting open. Before Steve could even fix his mouth to say anything, a shotgun blast knocked him out of his chair. Lisa stood in shock as she wiped the side of her face and her hand came away bloody. Alex kicked Lisa in her chest causing her to do a somersault out of the chair.

When Anthony and his boys finally realized what was going on it was too late. Victor already had his twin 45's trained on them. He smirked before taking their lives. When Victor returned back to the kitchen Lisa laid on the floor with a terrified look on her face. Victor roughly snatched Lisa up to her feet by her hair. "Where's the stash at?"

Lisa was too terrified to talk so she just cried. Victor sighed loudly as he head butted her breaking her nose spilling blood all over the place.

"We came all the way out to Alabama!" "Bitch you going to tell me something" Victor barked.

"You're wasting your time" Alex cut in. "She's too shaken up to talk right now. Do what you gotta do and let's go" he said exiting the house. As Alex walked back to the car he heard four shots ring out. He sat behind the wheel and waited for his brother to return back to the car. So far Montana had been setting up easy big paying jobs for them and Alex wasn't complaining. The only problems were the bodies. Every since the Gambino Brothers started working with Montana more bodies had been dropping left and right. Alex had enough money saved up and no longer wanted to kill and hurt people anymore. Alex's heart was no longer in it. He was going along for the ride and to make sure his brother was safe, but after tonight he had made up his mind he was officially done.

"Bitch should have just told us where the stash was" Victor said as he slid back in the passenger seat.

"I'm done with this shit Victor" Alex said pulling off. "I just can't do this anymore."

Victor laughed hysterically. "What are you talking about?"

"I'm done with this game" Alex said. "I want to live a regular life and enjoy my money before it's too late."

"Are you serious?"

"Dead serious" Alex said. "I want to start a family, get married, and go fishing. You know, regular people shit. All our life we had to struggle, steal, and fight for everything. Now it's time for us to just enjoy everything we worked so hard for."

"You bugging the fuck out" Victor said disappointed in his older brother. "What's next? You gonna want to give your life to Christ and get baptized or some shit?"

"Stop being so stubborn for once in your life" Alex said glancing over at his brother. "You need to quit this lifestyle too before it's too late. When we first started robbing people it was because we had no choice. It was either do or die, but we are rich now and we can't even enjoy it because we are too busy robbing and shooting people every night."

"You sounding like a bitch right now!" Victor shook his head in disgust. If his brother wanted to turn soft that was on him, but he wasn't going to stop doing what he did best. This was the only thing he knew how to do. For the rest of the ride the two brothers didn't say a word to one another. Alex felt as if his brother was being stupid for not realizing when enough was enough. The two had everything they could possibly want and need, but to Victor that still wasn't enough. The difference between the two brothers was that Alex did it for the money and Victor did it for the love of the sport. Victor felt as if his brother was turning soft. He loved his job and did it for the thrill and action. Of course the money was good, but in Victor's eyes he loved what he was doing so he didn't consider it work. So to hear his brother say what he said was shocking to him. Alex parked the stolen car on a low key street as he and Victor hopped out.

"So when we get back home what's your plan" Victor asked? "What you going to put all your money in the stock market and start smoking cigarettes with a cigarette holder?" He laughed.

"No, actually I'm going to go and live the good life" Alex told him.

"Something you and I never got a chance to do because we were always so busy looking for our next victim" he said. "We've been doing this for over fifteen years. I'm tired of doing the same ole shit. It's time for me to start doing new things."

"Sell out mufucka" Victor whispered. He wasn't trying to hear nothing his brother had to say. In his eyes his older brother had turned into a pussy.

"I've been looking at this nice house I think I'm going to buy it when we get back" Alex said. "Start owning some property and get on the right track. I'm gonna go on a few vacations and start enjoying some of this money we had to work so hard to get."

"Yeah whatever!" Victor waved his brother off. As far as Victor was concerned he didn't have anything else to say to his brother. When the two brothers reached the airport, Victor walked way ahead of Alex not wanting anything to do with him. Alex shook his head at how petty his brother was acting. He paid him no mind as he boarded the plane. Alex took a seat in the front of the plane while Victor sat in the back. Alex grabbed a magazine and began flipping through the pages. He needed something to help the time pass on the long flight and sleeping in public was something he never did, so the magazine was gonna have to do. Alex looked up from his magazine when he heard a soft woman's voice say. "Hey, how are you doing?"

"Hey" Alex said looking up at the beautiful black woman that sat in the seat next to him. The woman was in her mid-twenties, brown hair, slim, and long legs. She wore a regular pair of jeans, heels, and a woman's wife beater but she still looked good.

"You got enough room" Alex asked checking the woman out.

"Yes, thanks I'm fine" the woman replied also checking Alex out. The two went five minutes without say a word to the other until Alex decided to break the ice.

"So what's a pretty woman like you doing traveling all alone?"

"Last time I checked I was a grown woman," the woman replied. "And I know how to handle myself."

"So are you single," Alex said knowing that would bring a smile to the woman's face.

"Single and proud" the woman said proudly. "What about yourself?"

"I'm also single and proud" Alex replied. "I'm Alex" he said as he extended his hand.

"Peaches" the woman replied taking Alex's hand into hers. "So do you always try to pick up women on the plane?"

"Only beautiful ones" Alex said. In his line of work, he wasn't used to talking to woman often, so he was using his best game.

"Well today must be my lucky day" Peaches smiled. The man sitting next to her was handsome and she could tell that he was a nice person. She wouldn't mind getting to know him a little better. "So do you live in New York?"

"Yes what about yourself" Alex asked.

"Unfortunately" Peaches replied. "I'm currently living with my mother trying to save up enough money so I can move as far away from New York as possible."

"Moving out of New York might not be a bad idea" Alex said feeling her pain. Now that he was out of the game Alex wasn't sure what his next move was going to be. He had enough money to last him for a lifetime and no plans. Alex didn't know what his next move was, but one thing he did know was that he was going to have fun and enjoy himself in the process of spending his money. "When we land in New York would you care to join me for dinner?"

"I would love to" Peaches answered. "I'm starving."

Victor sat in the back of the plane thinking about how he was going to survive being a one man show. It was definitely going to be new to him, but Victor had confidence in himself and his gun. As long as he had his two 45's by side, he felt as if he were invincible. For the rest of the ride back to New York Victor made plans on what he was going to do since his brother had chickened out on him.

The Day Before

Jeezy sat in the brand new house he had just purchased. He looked around making sure everything was perfect. Paige was finally getting released from prison tomorrow and he wanted everything to be perfect when she came home. On the outside he looked regular, but on the inside he was super nervous. It had been so long since the two had lived together, that he wondered how it was going to be sleeping with her every night and waking up to her every morning again. Some nights he found himself still thinking about Pink. It had been two weeks since the last time they spoke . Jeezy wished things wouldn't have ended so ugly, but it was what is was.

Jeezy sat on the couch watching Sportcenter when he heard a light knock at the door. When Jeezy opened the door he sighed loudly when he saw Pink standing on the other side with several bags of groceries in her hands.

"What are you doing here and how did you find out where I moved to" Jeezy asked with a scowl on his face.

"You play too much" Pink said pushing past Jeezy. "I always know how to find my man. Now where do you want me to put these groceries?"

"Listen" Jeezy said grabbing Pink's arm firmly. "This is not a fucking joke! Don't just be popping up at my muthafucking house! I told you I was done with you!"

"You can't just wake up one morning and just break up with me cause you feel like it" Pink said looking him up and down. "It doesn't work like that."
As Jeezy sat there listening to her ramble at that very moment he regretted ever getting intimate with Pink. She definitely had a few screws loose. "Listen Paige will be home tomorrow and I can't have you just popping up" he told her. "Our thing was fun while it lasted, but now it's time to let it go."

Pink looked at Jeezy like he was speaking another language before she replied. "You play too much and I ain't got time for your playing hard to get. Now what do you want me to cook?" She said as she headed for the kitchen.

"Look bitch!" Jeezy grabbed her arm and spun her around so she could face him. "Take these fucking groceries and get the fuck out" he said forcing her back towards the door.

"You heartless bastard!" Pink screamed emotionally as she yanked her arm free and went crazy on Jeezy. She swung her arms wildly at his face trying to hit or scratch anything she could. Jeezy did his best to restrain her, but a few of her punches managed to slip through his guards catching him in his grill. Out of reflex Jeezy spun around and smacked Pink down to the floor.
She laid down on the floor looking up at him in shock holding the side of her face. "No you didn't just put your hands on me" she said in a harsh whisper.

"I'm sorry I didn't mean"
"You are going to wish you never did that" Pink said with fire in her eyes as she got up off the floor and left slamming the door behind her.

Jeezy looked at the door and shook his head. He had never put his hands on a woman before in his life. He felt bad about hitting Pink, but in all reality that's just what she needed. Jeezy picked up all the groceries from off the floor and finished preparing things so when Paige got home everything would be perfect. Jeezy didn't know what Pink had up her sleeve, but if she did anything to mess him and Paige's relationship up then she would have more to worry about than a slap.

Misery Loves Company

Victor drove around the city aimlessly sipping from his bottle of Barcardi 151. He couldn't believe his brother Alex had just up and quit on him leaving him out to dry. Not only that, but Victor had heard that his brother had just purchased a big house and was supposed to be in love with some woman he barely knew. Victor turned his bottle up, as he slowed down for a red light. All his life he had his brother by his side to watch his back, but now he felt like a child that had been given up for adoption at birth. "Fuck that" Victor said to himself as he busted a U-turn and headed towards his brother's new house. He had to go over there and see what was going on and definitely meet this new woman who had to be responsible for clouding his brother's judgment.

***

Alex and his new girlfriend Peaches sat over in the bar area of the house taking shots and sniffing lines of cocaine as Michael Jackson's classic song "Don't Stop 'Til You Get Enough" blasted through the speakers that were placed throughout the large house. Peaches was a very attractive looking dark skin chick in her mid-twenties. She was on the border line between fat and skinny. She worked a regular waitress job. Peaches may have been young, but she did genuinely love Alex, and every chance she got she made sure she showed him.
Alex knew his brother wouldn't approve of Peaches so that's why he wasn't in a rush to introduce her to him. Alex walked

around the house in a white wife beater and boxers while Peaches wore a black wife beater and a pair of black booty shorts.

"I love you so much baby" Peaches sang happily as she slid in Alex's arms and sloppily tongued kissed him. Alex gladly accepted her tongue as his hand explored her body.

"Not so fast" Peaches smiled as she pulled away from Alex. "I'mma go run the water for the hot tub" she said seductively.
"I'mma make you work tonight." She winked as she headed upstairs to the master bedroom's bathroom. Alex was just about to follow behind her until he heard the doorbell ring.

"What the fuck?" Alex said to himself stopping mid-stride. He never had company and nobody knew where he lived, but Peaches. He quickly grabbed his 38 from off the bar counter as he made his way to the door. Alex looked through the peephole and sucked his teeth when he saw who was on the other side. He loved his brother to death, but he knew his brother was coming by just to be nosey.

"Hey man what's up?" Alex asked opening the door. "What are you doing here?"

"What I need a reason to come visit my big brother?" Victor asked taking a quick swig from his bottle.

"Of course not; come on in" Alex said stepping to the side. When Victor stepped inside he looked around the large house.
"This is nice."

"Thanks" Alex smiled.

"You on your high horse I see" Victor laughed.

"What the fuck is that supposed to mean?" Alex huffed.

"You walking around here in this big ass house with all this fancy shit." Victor shook his head. "Living like a cracker!"

"So I'm on my high horse because I want to enjoy my money before it's too late" Alex asked matching his brother's tone. "I'm living like a cracker because I want nice things? You sound so stupid and ignorant."

"Oh I'm stupid and ignorant?" Victor repeated nodding towards the white powder that lay in a hundred dollar bill on top of the counter. "What the fuck is this? You know we don't fuck around with this shit!"

"Yeah not when we on the clock," Alex reminded him. "I'm officially retired meaning I'm free to do whatever the fuck I wanna do."

"You know what your problem is" Victor asked knocking the powder substance from off the top of the counter onto the floor.

"You one of them mufucka's that get money then don't know how to act."

"And let me guess; killing people for the hell of it is what you supposed to do when you got enough money to retire right" Alex said sarcastically. "Why can't you just be happy for me?" Alex knew his brother was just jealous that he had a new girlfriend and had not been spending much time with him lately. It had nothing to do with the house or the money.

"I am happy for you bro" Victor paused. "I just want things to be how they used to be."
Before Alex could reply, Peaches returned back down stairs and interrupted their conversation.

"Baby our water is ready." "Oh sorry I didn't know you had company."

"Come here baby." "I want you to meet somebody" Alex said. "This right here is my younger brother Victor."

"Hey Victor it's nice to meet you." "I've heard so much about you" Peaches said happily extending her hand.

Victor looked at Peaches like she smelled like sour milk as he turned and faced his brother. "Who's the bimbo?"

"This is my new girlfriend Peaches."
A smirk danced on Victor's lips. "But she's black!"

"So what if she black" Alex said quickly. "This is my girlfriend and I'm not going to let you disrespect her in my house."

"What do you know about this girl" Victor asked. "How you know she ain't a cop?"

"Because she's not" Alex answered quickly.

"Why because she told you she's not" Victor said looking Peaches up and down. It didn't matter what color her skin was, the truth was Victor wasn't going to like her regardless.
"I'mma leave you two alone so yall can talk" Peaches said as she headed back upstairs.

Once Peaches was out of ear shot, Victor continued. "You slipping bro. You got this chick clouding up your mind with all that powder. That's why you can't think straight."

"Is this what you came over here for" Alex said.

"Fuck it! You wanna be with that stupid bitch then so be it! I don't even care!"

Before Victor could finish his sentence Alex had already stole on him.

"Don't you ever disrespect me or my girl in my house" he said roughly escorting his younger brother to the door.

"Get the fuck off me!" Victor growled breaking free from his brother's grip. "You wanna be with her then fine by me, but when she fucks you over don't come calling me" he said storming out the front door.

Alex felt bad about having to put his hands on his little brother, but he knew if he didn't Victor would have kept on going, especially since he was drunk.

"Is everything alright" Peaches asked joining Alex back down stairs.

"Yes baby everything is fine" Alex said downing the liquid fire in one gulp. "I apologize for my brother's behavior tonight."
"No need to apologize" Peaches smiled. "He probably just misses his big brother."

"Yeah I bet." Alex knew his brother was jealous because Peaches was now in the picture, but he was no longer hungry and he didn't feel the need to be out in the streets putting in work so he decided to call it quits before someone else did it for him. On the flip side, Alex did feel a little bad about leaving his brother out to dry like that, but if he didn't separate himself when he did then he probably never would have ever been able leave the game when he did. Alex was just happy that he was able to leave on his own terms and not anybody else's.

**

Victor hopped out of his car and headed inside a popular bar. He desperately needed a drink. He couldn't believe his brother had picked a stranger over him and a woman at that. I guess it's true what they say, money does change people Victor thought as he ordered a drink at the bar. Victor scanned the place as he waited for the bartender to prepare his drink. It was a rowdy crowd, but it didn't matter to Victor because he didn't plan on being there long anyway.

Victor took his drink and took a seat at the end of the bar. A million thoughts ran through his mind as he sipped on his drink. His thoughts were immediately interrupted when he felt a light tap on his shoulder. Victor spun around on his bar stool and saw a beautiful woman before him.

"Hey sweetie is this seat taken?" The woman asked in a polite drunken slur.

"Nah go ahead, have a seat" Victor said looking up at the woman.

"Oh my God it's you!" The woman said staring at Victor like she had just seen a ghost. "HELP! SOMEBODY HELP ME!" the woman screamed.

"Hey calm down lady" Victor said standing to his feet.

"This man killed my brother and robbed him blind!" The woman screamed making a big scene. "Somebody call 911!"

"Fuck that I'm out" Victor said to himself as he headed for the exit.

"Hold it right there!" A white man barked with authority. "I'm an off duty cop." "Put your hands where I can see them" he ordered.
Victor ignored the man and kept it moving. As he walked he gripped the handle of his twin 45's.

"Hey somebody stop that man!" The off duty cop yelled as he jogged behind Victor.

As Victor approached the front door, a big bouncer stood in his way.

"Sir I can't let you leave right now" the bouncer's voice boomed. "Put your hands where" The bullet that exploded in his leg caused the bouncer to forget whatever it was he was trying to say. He immediately grabbed his thigh as he melted down to the floor. The echo from the gunshot sent the whole bar in a frenzy.
Victor quickly spun around and sent three shots into the off duty officer's chest dropping him where he stood. The off duty officer let off two shots before he slammed down to the floor. Victor quickly blended in with the crowd as he hurried out of the bar. Out in the parking lot Victor walked swiftly over to his car and hopped in. Once inside he held his arm that was bleeding badly. One of the shots that the off duty officer fired

had found a home in his arm. "Fuck!" Victor cursed, as he pulled off leaving the smell of burnt rubber in the air.

***

Alex laid in his king sized bed watching Sportscenter while Peaches slept with her head resting on his chest. After four rounds of hot sex Alex was also tired, but he couldn't sleep. Alex hated when he and his brother had disagreements. He just hoped his little brother would grow up one day.

Peaches jumped up out of her sleep when she heard somebody ringing their doorbell like they were crazy. "Who's ringing our doorbell like that" she asked with a scared look on her face.

"I don't know" Alex said as he hopped up and removed his shotgun from the closet. Peaches looked on in amazement at how fast, easy, and effortlessly he loaded the shotgun and got ready for action.

Alex flew down the steps skipping two at a time. His first instinct was to aim his shotgun at the door and blow whoever was on the other side to pieces, but he didn't want to murder someone in front of Peaches unless he had too. When Alex opened the door Victor spilled inside crashing to the floor.

"Mufucka caught me slipping" Victor slurred with a bloody smile on his face.
"Peaches get down here!" Alex yelled upstairs as he dragged his brother inside the house.

"Oh my God" Peaches said with her hands covering over her mouth when she saw how much blood was on the floor.

"Baby, help me get him up on the counter" Alex said, as he and Peaches struggled to get Victor on the counter top.

Victor grunted in pain as they placed his body up on the counter. "Call our street doctor."

"I got you" Alex replied, but on the inside he was furious. He didn't want Peaches to know anything about his past, but now she had seen and heard too much.

Alex ripped off Victor's shirt so he could try and find out where all the blood was coming from.

"None of this would have happened if you would have been watching my back tonight" Victor managed to say. "I blame you for this!"

Alex ignored his brother as he placed the call to their street doctor. He gave him the address and then hung up.

"You need me to do anything baby" Peaches asked.

"Yeah keep him awake while I go get rid of his car and if anybody knocks let them in" Alex said heading for the door.

"How do I keep him awake?"
"Talk to him" Alex said as he was stopped by Victor grabbing his arm.

"Don't leave me" Victor whispered.

"You can't be bringing shit like this to my house" Alex said scolding him like he was a child. "Keep that street shit in the streets" he said snatching his arm out of his brother's grip. "I have to go get this car out of my driveway just in case

somebody is looking for it and you lead them straight here!"
Alex huffed slamming the door behind him.

Once Alex left it was an awkward silence between Victor
and Peaches. Peaches knew Victor didn't like her so she didn't
know what to say.

"Does it hurt" she asked looking at the open wound on
Victor's shoulder.

"What the fuck you think" Victor said sarcastically. "Yeah
this shit hurts!"

"What happened?" "If you don't mind me asking" Peaches
said just wanting to keep him talking so he wouldn't pass out.

"I got shot because my brother wasn't there to watch my
back" Victor told her. "Ever since you came in the picture you
been fucking up his mind. I don't know what you doing to him,
but whatever it is you need to stop!"

"I'm not going to apologize for loving your brother"
Peaches said defensively. "You might as well get used to me
because I plan on being around for a while."
"Bitch" Victor barked. "I'll kill you before I let you take
my brother from me!" If he had the strength he probably
would have killed her right where she stood. Victor didn't like
who his brother was becoming and it was no way he was just
going to sit around and let some chick come mess up him and
Alex's relationship. He'd rather die before he let that happen.

Welcome Home

Jeezy stood outside in front of the jail leaning on the hood of his Range Rover. He had been waiting for Paige to be released for the past thirty minutes and each minute that passed seemed to feel like an hour. As Jeezy sat there waiting he wondered how it was going to be with Paige back home. Would she come out a whole new person? Would she be the same ole sweet loving person or had prison turned her into a cold hearted person who no longer cared about anything or anybody? Only time would tell. As Jeezy sat waiting he noticed two more cars pull up followed by a bus. He figured the inmates were finally about to be released. As Jeezy continued to wait, he felt his iPhone buzz in his pocket. He looked down at the screen and saw that he had a text message from Pink.

"Baby I know you are upset with me right now, but I just want you to know that I love you so much and I'm willing to play my position if you allow me back into your life. Please text me back or give me a call. Love Pink"

Jeezy quickly erased the message and slid his phone back into his pocket. He had been receiving text messages from her all throughout the night. Just as Jeezy was about to get impatient, he heard the door to the jail open and several women all walked out with big smiles on their faces.

Paige stepped out the prison wearing a black wife beater, a pair of black leggings, and some flip flops. Her hair was in a ponytail and her face had a special glow to it. The closer she got to Jeezy the bigger the smile on her face became. Paige had waited three whole years for this day to finally come. "What's up jailbird?" Jeezy smiled as Paige jumped in his arms and wrapped her legs around his waist trying to hug the life out of him. The two kissed for what seemed like thirty minutes straight before they decided to take a breath.

"Oh my fucking God" Paige said excitedly. "I'm so happy to be free!"

All Jeezy could do was smile as he pulled away from the jail. He was just so happy his queen was finally home. "So what's the first thing you want to do?"

"The first thing I need to do is go to a McDonalds," Paige smiled.
"I've been dying for a Big Mac and some fries."

After the two finished stuffing their faces at McDonalds, Jeezy took Paige to the spa so she could get the works. The next stop was the beauty parlor and then home.

As Jeezy sat listening to Paige talk he felt his iPhone buzz in his pocket again. He looked at the screen and saw that it was another text message from Pink.

"If you think you are getting rid of me that easy, you got another thing coming!"

Jeezy erased the message and slid his phone back in his pocket as he pulled into the driveway.

"Dammmmmn!" Paige said with a big smile. "This is our new house?"

"Yup" Jeezy said tossing Paige her own set of keys. Paige caught the keys and hurried towards the front door. When she made it through the front door, she couldn't believe her eyes. "It's beautiful" she whispered.

Jeezy lead her upstairs to the bathroom where he ran her a nice bubble bath in their hot tub. He washed Paige's body from top to bottom while he listened to her talk. When Jeezy reached the scar on Paige's stomach where she had been stabbed, he bent down and kissed it. "I'm sorry you had to go through all that because of me."

Paige smiled. "Trust me you are more than worth it and if I could change how everything played out" she paused. "I wouldn't change one thing."

When Paige got out of the tub Jeezy dried her off and gently laid her across the bed.
"Baby, I"

"Shhhh" Jeezy whispered as he spread Paige's legs apart and began kissing her clit. Jeezy had been waiting three years to taste her fruit and now that she was finally home he planned on enjoying it. He licked and sucked all over Paige's pussy causing her to make loud moans and screams. Her orgasm came hard and fast. It was a series of waves and then a devastating orgasm erupted and Jeezy was right there to catch all of it. For the rest of the night Jeezy and Paige had wild sex.

***

The next morning Jeezy woke up to the sound of his iPhone ringing. He sat up and looked around. He noticed that Paige wasn't in the bed. He picked up his phone to answer it and noticed the number was blocked.

"Who is this?"

"You know exactly who this is," was the reply.

"What do you want from me?" Jeezy huffed.

"Did you and your "Queen" have a good time last night" Pink asked with jealousy dripping from her voice.

"What is your problem" Jeezy asked in a harsh whisper. "We had our fun, made a lot of money in the process, and now it's over so deal with it!"

"I ain't dealing with shit" Pink said in a nasty tone. "How can you just get rid of me so easy like that? As if I never existed to you?"
Jeezy could hear her tears through the phone. "Listen Pink from day one I told you what it was."

"You used me!"

"I didn't use you" Jeezy replied quickly.

"You used me as a stepping stone until Paige got out so now that she's home I'm useless to you" Pink said. "I took care of your black ass for three whole years. I put you on the map and this is how you do me; really?"

"Listen bitch" Jeezy began. "First of all you ain't put me on the map. I been on the map! Second of all you ain't give me shit. I was right there in the strip club with you every night earning my half. So you can miss me with that bullshit!"

"Can we please talk face to face" Pink begged.
"No!"

"Please? You at least owe me that much."

"I don't owe you shit" Jeezy said simply.

"I'm going to kill Paige!" Pink snapped. "I'm going to kill her in front of you and let you watch. You think you just gone use me for three years and then kick me to the curb like I'm trash? I don't think so!"

Jeezy hung up in Pink's face. He had heard enough foolishness for one morning. Just as he hung up his phone Paige walked into the bedroom carrying breakfast.

"I know you haven't had breakfast in bed in three years so I figured I'd hook you up." Paige smiled.

"Thanks baby! You are the greatest!" Jeezy returned her smile.

"Baby can I ask you a question" Paige asked while sitting down next to Jeezy.

"Sure, you ask me anything you want."

"How did you get the money for this big house and all these nice things" Paige asked.

Jeezy shoved a piece of turkey bacon in his mouth before he replied. "While you were away I was working with this stripper chick" he began. "We sold a shit load of E pills and we had our hand in a little prostitution. I did what I had to do for us."

"Are you still dealing with her?"

"Dealing with who" Jeezy asked playing dumb.

"The stripper; are you still dealing with her" Paige asked making herself crystal clear.

"Nah I cut her off" Jeezy said. "I knew you probably wouldn't feel comfortable with me having to be around her all day so I ended our business relationship before you came home" he told her.

"Thank you for being honest with me baby" Paige said leaning over and kissing Jeezy on the lips. "So many nights I sat up in jail wondering what you were out here doing."

"This is what I've been doing" Jeezy said sweeping his hand thru the air. "I have been setting things up so when you got home you could be more than comfortable." He knew when Paige was released from jail she was going to have a million questions about what he had been doing while she was away so he was already prepared.

"The whole time you were away all I did was think about you" Jeezy told her. "Now that you are home, I'm never letting you out of my sight."

Not knowing what to say or do Paige just gave Jeezy a big kiss and hugged him tightly. "Thank you baby" she whispered in his ear.

"No need to thank me baby" Jeezy said as he dug into his food.

For the rest of the day Jeezy and Paige had sex a few times and cuddled up under each other watching all of the movies that Paige had missed while she was in jail.

"I want to go out tonight" Paige said sitting up.

"What do you wanna do? Do you wanna go out to eat or something?"

"Nah I want to go to a club," Paige smiled. "It's been a while since I went out and enjoyed myself."

"That's cool baby. I don't mind if you go out and enjoy yourself" Jeezy said.

Paige laughed. "No I want you to come with me."

An hour later Jeezy parked his Benz in the clubs parking lot and let the engine die.

Paige stepped out of the Benz wearing a short black dress with a pair of black sexy 4 inch heels to match. She wore her hair up in a bun with a nice pair of earrings to help bring out her outfit.

Jeezy hopped out the Benz also wearing all black. He wore a black button up shirt, a pair of black jeans, and some black Prada sneakers.

Inside the club was packed from wall to wall with drunken people all having a good time. Jeezy and Paige squeezed their way over to the bar. After a few drinks Paige hit the dance floor with Jeezy. The two grinded close up on one another as their bodies swayed perfectly to the beat.

"Baby I need a break" Jeezy smiled walking away from the dance floor.

"Let me find out you getting old" Paige laughed. Her body was covered in sweat, but she didn't mind because she was having fun with the love of her life. She couldn't believe how the simplest things put a smile on her face. All this time she had been taking her freedom for granted and not a appreciating it, but the new Paige planned on enjoying every minute of the rest of her life.

"I'm going to get us some more drinks" Jeezy said disappearing in the direction of the bar.

Paige stood in place doing her two-step when she felt someone grind up behind her. She smiled thinking it was Jeezy, but when she felt the aggressive grab on her hips with a pair of strong hands, immediately she knew it wasn't Jeezy. Paige spun around and saw a chubby man who wore a thin goatee standing in front of her.

"Mmm...mmm...mmm" the man hummed as he eyed Paige up and down with a perverted look in his eyes. "The world must be about to end cause I'm damn sure looking at an angel" the man began with his whack Mack Daddy game. "If this is a dream then I don't want to wake up."

"My man is right over there" Paige said still laughing at the man's whack game. "So if you don't want to wake up on the floor, then I suggest you keep it moving."

"We can't have a friendly conversation because you have a man" the chubby man asked in a drunken slur. "I was just trying to give you a compliment."

"Thank you for the compliment." Paige smiled politely. "One hug and I'm gone" the chubby man said as he pulled Paige in close for a hug.

"Chill" Paige huffed trying to push the big man back, but his strength and size easily over powered her.

"Just one hug baby" the chubby man barked. His tone growing more aggressive with each word he spoke. His hands slid down to Paige's ass as he palmed both of her cheeks with ease.

The chubby man leaned in for a kiss until he felt a hard blow to the side of his head that caused him to drop down to his knees.

Jeezy stood over the chubby man and rained blow after blow on the drunken man's face until two bouncers finally came and roughly escorted him up out the club. One bouncer had Jeezy in a choke hold while the other held his legs and carried him through the club.

"Put him down. He didn't even do anything" Paige yelled at the bouncers trying to remove their hold from her man. Once outside the bouncers tossed Jeezy out on the concrete like he was a piece of trash. Jeezy quickly bounced back up to his feet ready to go at the bouncers,until Paige stood in front of him.

"No baby let's just go home; please" she cried. "We don't need any more problems."

Fire danced in Jeezy's eyes as he backed away staring a hole in the two bouncers. His first thought was to go to his Benz grab his 40 caliber and wet up the whole club, but the scared and nervous look on Paige's face forced him to rethink things.

When they made it back to the Benz Paige hugged Jeezy tightly.

"Thank you for not over reacting" she whispered. "We already spent enough time away from each other and I don't ever wanna have to do that again."

"I understand baby" Jeezy said as he hopped behind the wheel and headed home.

***

For the past month Victor had been staying in Alex's house until his shoulder finally healed up. He still couldn't believe the way his brother had been acting. Victor tried his hardest to stay out of Peaches way, but some how the two always seemed to bump into each other.

Victor sat on the couch loading up his twin 45's when he noticed Peaches make her way over to the kitchen. When the two made eye contact Victor shook his head in disgust.

"What is your problem" Peaches said finally fed up with Victor's nasty attitude. "I've done nothing to you for you to be acting this way to me.I mean why can't we both just get along?"

"Get along?" Victor echoed standing to his feet. "Bitch you stole my brother away from me and turned him into a bitch, then after all of that you have the nerve to ask me why can't we get along?"

"Victor I didn't steal anyone from anybody" Peaches began. "Why is it so wrong that your brother wants to change his life around? I guess it's true what they say misery does love company."

Victor chuckled. He couldn't stand Peaches. In his eyes she was nothing but a nasty gold digger who was just enjoying a free ride off of Alex's hard earned money and Victor wasn't just going to sit there and let her take the only family he had left away from him.

"My brother might not know what you're up too, but I see right through yo ass like glass."

"What are you talking about" Peaches asked confused. "I have nothing but love for your brother. The sooner you figure that out the better off we will be." What Peaches was saying got cut off when she heard the doorbell ring. She got up, but Victor quickly stopped her.

"Don't bother." "It's for me" he said bopping over towards the door. Victor opened the door and on the other side stood a well-dressed prostitute.

"Hey baby" the prostitute smiled as she stepped inside the nice house wearing a tight fitting one piece red mini skirt and some red pumps. "My name is Cinnamon" she said licked her lips. "How can I please you?"
"Hold up" Peaches interfered. "What do you thinks going on up in here?"

"Mind your fucking business" Victor huffed as he continued to check Cinnamon out from head to toe. Peaches sucked her teeth as she rushed upstairs to go inform Alex what was going on down stairs.

Victor pulled Cinnamon down onto his lap, as his hands began to explore her curvy voluptuous body.

Upstairs Alex was in the middle of his daily workout when he saw Peaches bust up in the room. "You won't believe what your brother is downstairs doing" she huffed.

Alex sighed loudly as he hopped up off the floor from his push-up position. "What is he doing now?"

"He downstairs with a prostitute right now in our living room"
"A prostitute" Alex huffed as he slid a wife beater over his head and headed downstairs.

Downstairs Victor sat on the couch tossing a few singles as he watched Cinnamon strip for him. "That's right baby shake that shit" he smiled.

"How are you doing miss" Alex said politely. "I'm sorry but you have to leave" he said helping to pick up Cinnamon's clothes from off the floor.

"Man what are you doing" Victor said standing to his feet.
Alex ignored his brother as he escorted Cinnamon out of his house.
"Damn why did you do that" Victor spat. "I paid her in full already."

"Get your shit" Alex said in a serious tone. He could no longer take his brother staying with him. He knew Victor was only acting like this because of Peaches.

"What do you mean get my shit?"

"You gotta go" Alex told him. "If you can't respect me and who I choose to live with then you gotta go!"

"So" Victor smirked. "This is what it's come down to huh? Your own brother; the only family you ever had or some new chick who you just met and you choose her over me."

"I didn't choose anybody" Alex corrected him. "You need to grow up. Sooner or later you're going to find a nice woman that you like and instead of being mean to her, I'm going to embrace her and accept her into the family."

Victor chuckled. "You are a real piece of work" he said bumping shoulders with Alex as he walked out the house.

"It doesn't have to be like this you know" Alex said from the door way.

Victor ignored his brother's words as he hopped in his car and pulled off. As far as he was concerned he no longer had a brother. Anyone that would choose a woman over family was no family of his.

Alex closed the door and let out a deep breath. He couldn't believe how childish and jealous his brother was acting over him having a girlfriend. It was no way Alex was going to choose between the only two people he had in his life and if Victor didn't like it then so be it.

You Gotta Be Kidding Me

Jeezy woke up and noticed he was in the bed alone. This wasn't nothing new. Every morning since Paige was released from jail she always brought Jeezy breakfast in bed and today was no different. Jeezy hopped out the bed and sniffed the turkey bacon filled air as he went in the bathroom to brush his teeth and take a quick shower.

Jeezy hopped out the shower and threw on a pair of sweat pants and a wife beater. Then he headed downstairs to join Paige. The closer Jeezy made it to the bottom of the steps he heard more than one voice coming from the living room. When Jeezy made it in the living room his stomach immediately leaped up to his throat when he saw Pink sitting on the couch next to Paige.

"Hey baby" Paige said happily. "I was just making us some breakfast when our new next door neighbor came over to say hi."

"Nice to meet you I'm April" Pink said extending her hand.

Jeezy shook her hand with a weird uncomfortable look on his face. He couldn't believe that Pink was actually sitting right there in his living room.

"I was just making some breakfast. Would you care to join us" Paige asked. "It's more than enough."

"No I couldn't" Pink said putting up a weak protest.

"It will be great. Then we can get to know each other a little better" Paige said as she disappeared into the kitchen.

Once the coast was clear Jeezy firmly grabbed Pink's arm. "What the fuck are you doing here?"

"I know you ain't think you were just going to get rid of me that easy. Especially after you told me you loved me."

"What," Jeezy said confused. "I never told you I loved you!"
"Not verbally, but your actions said "damn Pink I love you so much and you are the one for me." She smiled. "You are going to continue to be with me or else I'm going to tell your precious Paige everything" Pink threatened. "I just moved in next door so it ain't any excuses. I expect my dick at least four times a week."

"Okay the food is ready" Paige said appearing out of nowhere.

At the kitchen table Jeezy ate his breakfast silently as Pink and Paige talked as if they had known each other for years. Jeezy didn't know how, but some how he was going to have to get rid of Pink and do it quickly before things got too out of hand.

"So how long have you two been together" Pink asked sipping on her orange juice.

"Since forever" Paige answered proudly.

"Well maybe Jeezy here can hook me up with one of his friends." Pink laughed knowing he didn't deal with a lot of people.

While sitting at the table, Pink held her phone under the table and texted Jeezy. "Meet me next door at my house in 10 minutes. The back door is open."

Jeezy read the message and quickly finished his food. "Baby I'll be right back I gotta run out for a second" he said leaning down kissing Paige on the lips.

"Okay baby be careful" Paige said. "If you come back and I'm not here I'm at the hair salon" she told him as he headed out the door. Pink made small talk for the next 15 minutes before she decided it was time for her to leave. "Girl come over anytime and don't be a stranger" Pink said as she hugged Paige and kissed her on the cheek and then left.

***

Pink walked in her new house and saw Jeezy leaning on the counter by the kitchen sipping on a glass of wine.

"Hey daddy make yourself at home" Pink said kicking off her heels as she came up out of her one piece skirt and tossed it on the arm of the couch. "I missssssssed you" she said sliding in for a hug.

"What is this all about" Jeezy said denying her access for a hug.

"Why can't you just let me go?"

"Why; so the next bitch can get the wonderful man it took so long for me to build?" "I don't think so" she laughed.

"You sound ridiculous!" Jeezy shook his head in disgust. "So what you going to follow me everywhere I move to?"

"Sho is" Pink said with her hands on her hips. "Why can't you see that I love you with all my heart and no other chick including Paige can or will take care of you better or treat you better than I would?" She truly loved Jeezy and wanted to spend the rest of her life with him. "You know you love me so I don't know why you fronting?"

"Fronting?" Jeezy repeated. "Listen! What we did was fun while it lasted, but now all that is over with. Paige and I are going to get married."

Pink laughed. "Over my dead body" she said with a crazy looking smile on her face as she unbuckled Jeezy's belt buckle and aggressively snatched his pants down.

"No!" Jeezy said pushing Pink's face away from his crotch.

"This is my dick" Pink said with a firm grip on Jeezy's manhood.

"Now give me my shit before I go next door and tell Paige what the real reason is why I moved next door."

With no other options all Jeezy could do was stand there while Pink slowly sucked and licked all over his dick. His mind might not have been into it, but his dick had a mind of its own. Jeezy fucked Pink's mouth as if he was mad at her. Pink grabbed his butt cheeks forcing him even further in her mouth until he finally exploded.

Jeezy put his clothes back on and then headed for the front door until Pink cleared her throat and stopping him. "What now" Jeezy asked with an attitude as he turned to look at Pink.

"Where the fuck you think you going" Pink said as she laid back on the counter and opened her legs. "If you know what's best for you; you better get over here and eat this good pussy."

Jeezy sighed loudly as he walked over to the counter and looked down at Pink's fat shaved, wet pussy. Jeezy buried his face in between Pink's legs as he orally pleased her.

Pink moaned loudly as she held on to the back of Jeezy's head as he forced her to cum for him yet again.
An hour later once Pink was finished with Jeezy she kicked him out. "Same time tomorrow" she said slamming the door behind him. Satisfied with the work Jeezy had put in Pink went and hopped in her hot tub and began thinking of other ways to make Jeezy's life miserable.

Change of Heart

Alex sat on the couch in his living room in the middle of the night watching Scarface. As he watched the movie his mind drifted off to his brother. He missed Victor and he knew eventually his brother would end up dead or in jail if he continued to let him go on missions alone. Not to mention that Alex was getting bored just sitting in the house all the time and living a regular life. His whole life had been filled with action and now he was beginning to miss his old life.

"Hey" Peaches said standing at the bottom of the stairs. "Want some company?" Alex smiled and patted the seat cushion next to him. "What's on your mind baby" Peaches asked curling up next to Alex.

"I was thinking about getting back in the game."

"Huh" Peaches said sitting straight up. "Back in the game? Why? For what?"

"My brother needs me" Alex told her. "I have a bad feeling something real bad is going to happen to him if I'm not there to watch his back."

"I need you too Alex" Peaches shouted as her eyes began to water. "Just because he wants to throw his life away doesn't mean you have to throw yours away with him."

"But..."

"Ain't no buts" Peaches cut him off. "Instead of worrying about your brother, you should be thanking God that after all the shit you been through you're still here safe and sound. Be smart Alex" she pleaded. "That heartless killer ain't you no more. This is the real Alex" she said jabbing her index finger in his chest.

Alex knew what Peaches was saying was right, but she wasn't in his shoes and would never understand.

"Please baby I need you" Peaches whispered. "This is your chance to move on from that life. You made it out by the Grace of God so why would you want to go backwards? That doesn't make any sense."

Alex knew Peaches wouldn't understand where he was coming from, but he knew Victor would be done if he didn't save him from himself.

"I hate to have to do this" Peaches stood up. "But it's either going to be me or your brother!" The silence that came after the question was all the answer Peaches needed. "Fine" she said making her way back upstairs.

Alex continued to finish watching Scarface as he wondered if he was making the right decision or signing his death certificate.

An hour later Peaches struggled downstairs with a big suitcase and a duffle bag over her shoulder.

"Baby you don't have to do this" Alex said hoping Peaches would stay.

"I refuse to stay and watch you go out on a suicide mission. If you want to go out and get yourself killed by all means, but I'm not just going to sit around until something bad happens."

"Don't go baby!" "I love you" Alex said knowing that if Peaches left she wasn't coming back.

"If you did I wouldn't be leaving right now" Peaches said in a low tone as she kissed Alex on the cheek and left him standing right there. Alex stood in the door way until Peaches taillights disappeared down the street. Alex knew the choice he was making wasn't the wisest one, but it was what he had to do. He closed the door and pulled out his cell phone and dialed Victor's number.

***

Victor stood over the body of a teenaged boy whose hands were tied behind his back with duct tape. He had been torturing the boy for the last fifteen minutes trying to get him to tell him where his father's stash was. When Victor rushed inside the house he noticed that no one was home except for the teenage boy. In the streets his father was called Hov and was a major player in the game. Word on the streets was that Hov was sitting on a nice lump sum of money. From the looks of the big house Victor knew that everything he heard about Hov was true.

"Please don't hurt me" the boy pleaded scared to death. He didn't know why the man standing over him wanted to hurt him or why he was even there.

"Shut the fuck up" Victor said kicking the boy in his face. The boy's head violently jerked back from the impact as blood began to spill from his nose. Victor pulled out one of his 45's and put a bullet in the boy's leg making sure he didn't move while he went and searched the house.

***

Hov pulled his 745 B.M.W up in his driveway and killed the engine. He and his main henchman Alpo were coming to take Hov's son the Knicks game.

"Yo I hope you ready" Hov shouted as he entered his home. "The game starts in an hour" he said grabbing two Heinekens from the fridge and handing one to Alpo. When Hov stepped foot in the living room and saw his son sprawled out across the floor leaking he couldn't believe his eyes. He immediately rushed over and kneeled by his side. "Go check the house" he said over his shoulder to Alpo as he dialed 911.

Alpo removed his 16 shot 9mm and slowly made his way upstairs.

***

Upstairs Victor dumped a box full of woman's jewelry into a shopping bag when he heard the door slam followed by a grown man's voice. Victor quickly pulled out his twin 45's making his way out into the hallway. Soon as he stepped out the bedroom he saw a man to his right trying to creep up the steps. Victor immediately opened fired as he back peddled down the hallway. Alpo quickly took cover behind the banister on the stairs as he returned a few reckless shots over his shoulder.

"Shit!" Hov cursed when he heard a gunfight erupt upstairs. He quickly pulled his 38 from the small of his back and made his way upstairs.

Victor popped shot after shot with a gun in each hand before disappearing in one of the bedrooms. Alpo slowly made his way down the hallway. This was the type of shit he lived for. Action should have been his middle name. He slowly entered the room he saw the gunman enter and quickly ran over towards the open window. When Alpo looked out the window he saw Victor hopping over the next door neighbor's fence. He aimed his 9mm at the fence and opened fire hoping to catch one of Victor's body parts.

Seconds later Hov entered the room with a two handed grip on his 38. "Where'd he go?"

"That pussy jumped out the window" Alpo said jamming a fresh clip in the base of his 9mm.

"Did you see that mufuckas face" Hov asked.

Alpo smiled. "Of course I did."

***

Victor kept peeking up at his rearview mirror as he drove down the street. Things were much harder for him without Alex there to watch his back. Now Victor was more paranoid than ever. Without Alex by his side he felt naked, but one man didn't stop the show. As Victor drove he heard his cell phone ringing. He looked down at the screen and saw Alex's name flashing across the screen. "What" he answered.
"Your brother is back!" "Meet me at my crib" Alex said ending the call. A big smile appeared on Victor's face as he put his phone down and made a U-turn towards his brother's crib.

Never Be The Same

***

Alex stood in his kitchen having a drink when he saw Victor walk through his front door with a smile on his face.

"Finally I see you decided to come to your senses" Victor said giving his brother a warm hug.

"What you thought I was just going to sit back and let you have all the fun" Alex replied with a smile.

"What happened with Peaches" Victor asked.

"Had to kick her to the curb" Alex admitted.

"You didn't need her anyway" Victor said. "All we'll ever need is each other. Together can't nobody stop us."

Victor's cell phone ringing interrupted the two's moment. He answered his phone and replied with nothing but two word answers. "What time? How much? No problem" he said before ending the call.

"Who was that?" Alex asked.

"That was Montana and he said he has a real big job for us tomorrow." Victor smiled. "You ready to get your feet wet again?"

"I was born ready" Alex smiled.

Really Tho

Jeezy sat on the couch in his living room playing Madden while Jay-Z and Kanye West's album "Watch The Throne" pumped through the surround sound system. For the past month Pink had Jeezy eating right out of the palm of her hands. He continued to give her what she wanted so he could protect Paige's heart. He knew if Paige found out that he was fucking Pink while she was away she would definitely go through the roof. In the last month Paige and Pink had become the best of friends. They spent a lot of time together and when the two wasn't together they were on the phone or either texting one another. Jeezy wanted to just come straight out and tell Paige the truth, but the fear of losing her in the process was the only thing that stopped him. As Jeezy sat playing video games he heard a light knock at the front door. He got up and looked through the peephole and immediately he knew it was about to be trouble when he saw Pink standing on the other side of the door.

"What do you want" Jeezy asked cracking the door.

"You know exactly what I want" Pink whispered seductively.

"Where's Paige?"

"She's not here" Jeezy told her. Once Pink heard that, she pushed her way into the house and leaned in and kissed Jeezy on the lips.

143

"I've been thinking about my dick all day" Pink said tugging at Jeezy's belt buckle.

"Chill" he said smacking Pink's hands away as he backed up into the kitchen. "Paige will be back any minute."

"Fuck Paige!" Pink hated the fact that Jeezy just up and stopped loving her when Paige got out of prison. Even though Paige never actually did anything to her, Pink still hated Paige for taking away the best thing she ever had. "This dick belongs to me!" She reminded Jeezy as she unbuckled his pants and had her way with his dick. Pink deep throated Jeezy's dick and let it slid in and out of her mouth as she gagged loving every second of it. Pink gave Jeezy's dick one last slurp as she stood up, turned around, and bent over the counter. Jeezy lifted up Pink's short skirt and saw that she didn't have any panties.

Jeezy looked up at the clock on the wall and knew that Paige would be walking through the front door any second. He quickly entered Pink from behind and banged her out from behind hoping he came fast this go around. With each stroke Pink threw her big round ass back screaming to the top of her lungs with each stroke. Jeezy knew she was just screaming loudly like that in hopes that when Paige pulled up in the driveway she would hear them. With each stroke Jeezy delivered he watched as Pink's ass cheeks jiggled and bounced all over the place. All that could be heard throughout the house was Pink's loud cries and skin smacking against each other. Jeezy pumped away until he finally exploded all over her ass. He quickly pulled his pants up and wiped his semen off of Pink's ass with a paper towel.

"You got what you wanted now leave" Jeezy said pointing at the door. Before Pink could reply she and Jeezy's head turned towards the front door as they watched Paige walk through the front door with a hand full of bags.

"Hey girl what are you doing here" Paige asked giving Pink a hug followed by a kiss on the cheek.

"I came over here to see if you and Jeezy wanted to go party with me tonight" Pink said laughing to herself knowing she had just finished fucking the shit out of Paige's man right in her kitchen.

"Yeah that sounds good to me" Paige said. "I just bought a few new outfits."

"Why are you going on a job interview or something?" Pink asked nosily.

"No I got my first audition for this new movie next week and I'm so nervous" Paige said honestly. "It feels like forever since I've been in front of a camera."

"Don't worry about it baby, you going to do fine" Jeezy told her.

"Yeah I know you will do fine as well" Pink smiled. "If you want I can come over and help you with your lines if that will help?"

"Awww thanks April that's so nice of you" Paige said.

"That's what friends are for" Pink said heading for the front door.

"I'll be back in an hour and yall better be ready" she said closing the door behind her.

"She is such a nice woman" Paige said as she headed upstairs to try on her new outfits.

***

Pink and Paige entered the club with Jeezy bringing up the rear. Jeezy felt like a puppet on a string; the way he was doing everything and anything that Pink asked of him so Paige wouldn't find out about their relationship and be heart broken. He knew Paige wouldn't leave him if she found out, but their relationship would never be the same and slowly the two would fall apart. That was something Jeezy couldn't allow to happen.

Jeezy sipped on a drink while he watched Pink and Paige enjoy their selves. In his mind he wondered just how far Pink was willing to go with this whole game. As Jeezy sat in the cut watching Paige he noticed two men approach Pink and Paige. He knew his woman was fine so when guys tried to holla at her it didn't bother him. Besides he knew Paige would never disrespect him with another guy.

"You are looking good enough to eat right now ma, who you up in here with?" The handsome man who stood before Pink asked.
"I'm in here by myself" Pink smiled. "You got a name?"
"Everyone calls me Hov" the man said with a smile.
"Well everyone calls me Pink" she said as the two shook hands.

"So you party a lot" Alpo asked checking out Paige's ass. She was definitely the kind of chick that he would smash.
"No not really" Paige answered. She knew Jeezy was in the club and didn't want it to look like she was giving Alpo some play so she kept her answers short and sweet.

"What's good you tryna hang out after the club" Alpo pressed.

"No thank you" Paige said politely. "My man is right over there" she nodded over towards Jeezy.

"That clown got you on lockdown like that?" Alpo laughed as he walked off leaving Paige standing there.

When Paige made her way back over to the bar where Jeezy stood he quickly handed her a drink.

"Well it sure looks like April is having a good time" Paige said as they watched her and the guy she had just met getting busy on the dance floor.

Hov palmed Pink's ass as the two danced closely. Pink loved how Hov took control. She could tell he was boss and not to mention his confidence was a straight turn on. "Let's take this party back to my place."

"What you think you got it like that or something?" Pink smiled with one hand on her hip.

"You already know" Hov winked.

"Let me go tell my girlfriend I'm about to leave" Pink said making her way over to the bar. When Pink made it over to the bar she smiled as she turned and faced Paige. "I'm going to catch up with y'all later. I think I just found Mr. Right" she smiled shooting Jeezy a private look.

"Handle your business girl" Paige gave her a high five.

"Okay I'll get up with y'all tomorrow" Pink said disappearing through the crowd.

Never Be The Same

As Jeezy watched Pink snake her way through the crowd, he prayed that whoever this new guy was would steal Pink's heart so he wouldn't have to deal with the crazy bitch anymore.

Too Good To Be True

The Gambino brothers entered Montana's office and helped themselves to a seat. Montana had been bugging them about this big job, but wouldn't give any details over the phone.

"So what's up" Victor asked leaning back in his seat.

"I got a big job for you two" Montana smiled. "It's a simple job. All yall have to do is follow instructions."

"If it's so simple then why do you need us to do it" Alex asked suspiciously.

"Because you two were born for jobs like this" Montana smiled. "The job is simple. It's this big house downtown and word on the streets is it's the stash house of some cat named Hov. A little birdie told me that he and his team went on vacation for the weekend."

"So the house is just sitting there filled with money inside" Alex asked.

"Absolutely" Montana smiled. "I want you two to go it and bring it back."

"Deal" Victor said quickly thinking about the big payday. "What's the address?"

Montana slid a piece of paper across his desk to Victor. "This job is going to be a piece of cake."

"See you later on tonight" Victor said as he and Alex got up and made their exit.

Back in the car Alex stopped Victor before he pulled off. "I don't like how this sounds."

"What you mean this going to be like taking candy from a baby" Victor said pulling out of the parking spot.

"If this job was going to be so easy then why does Montana need us to do it?"

"Stop being paranoid all the time" Victor huffed.

"Whatever we take from this house, we are keeping! Fuck Montana I don't trust him" Alex said seriously.

"Relax" Victor said. "We been doing business with Montana for months and he hasn't steered us wrong yet."

Victor pulled up in front of the address that Montana had given him.

"Ride pass" Alex said so he could scope the house out first.

"What you think?" Victor asked as rain started to pour down.

"It looks quiet" Alex said. "I say we bring the big boys out for this one.

Victor parked the car a block away from the house and popped the trunk. Alex grabbed an Uzi from out the trunk and handed Victor a Tech-9.

Alex didn't know what it was about the house, but something just didn't feel right. Victor shot the lock off the front door and lifted his leg and kicked it open. Inside was quiet just as Montana said it would be.

"Told you this shit was going to be a piece of cake" Victor smirked making his way through the house.

"Let's find this money and get up outta here" Alex said.

As the Gambino Brothers walked through the house Alex stopped dead in his tracks when he heard several cars coming to sharp stops right in front of the house. "What the fuck?" Alex whispered as he walked over to the window and peeked through the blinds. Outside Hov, Alpo, and seven cars full of goons with automatic weapons prepared to run up in the house after the Gambino Brothers.

"Looks like we've got company" Alex announced. "That mufucka Montana set us up!"

"What are you talking about?" Victor asked as he peeked through the blinds and spotted the man he had a shootout with the other night. Just the thought of Montana setting them up pissed Victor off. In a quick motion he ripped down the blinds and opened fire on the small army straight through the window.

Hov quickly took cover behind one of the vehicles as he loaded up his A.K. Usually a boss didn't go to war with his troops, but this was personal. Hov quickly sprung up from behind the car and opened fire on the house. The gun rattled in his hands as he waved his arms back and forth as he walked up to the front door. Alpo was the first man inside follow by a few other goons. Hov pushed all the men to the side as he cautiously made his way through the living room. He gave a silent signal to Alpo to follow him upstairs while the other soldiers took the downstairs.

Hov swallowed hard as he slowly made his way upstairs. Once his foot hit the top step he heard a loud series of gunshots coming from downstairs followed by loud screams. Hov and Alpo quickly dashed back downstairs only to find five of their men sprawled out across the floor.

"Stop all this fucking hiding!" Alpo yelled squeezing the trigger on his machine gun. When he let go of his trigger Victor sprung up from behind the counter and opened fire on Hov and Alpo. The two men quickly dashed in opposite directions to avoid getting their heads blown off.

"Let's go" Alex said as he opened fire so Victor could escape through the back door. Once the coast was clear Alex quickly followed in his brother's footsteps.

When Hov and Alpo finally made it outside it was too late all that could be seen were headlights flying down the street. "Fuck!" Hov cursed because he knew he had just missed his best chance at killing both brothers at the same time.

Out of Hand

Pink laid in her king sized bed on the phone talking to Paige while Jeezy was eating her pussy. Jeezy felt bad for what he was doing but what other choices did he have?

"Yeah girl I'll be over there in a few I just got to take care of a little unfinished business" Pink said ending the call. Once she hung up the phone she gyrated her hips further into Jeezy's face until she released on his face. Satisfied with his work Pink dismissed Jeezy as if he was trash. "Okay now get the fuck out! When I need my pussy and ass ate again I'll give you a ring."

"This stops today" Jeezy said wiping his mouth with the back of his hand. "Before I let you take advantage of me any longer I'd rather tell Paige about us myself."

"If you don't continue to give me what I want, I'll kill Paige" Pink threatened. Jeezy slowly walked up to Pink until they were face to face.

"Bitch if you ever come close to her again I'll kill you myself" Jeezy said sternly. "That ain't a threat!"

"We'll have to see about that now won't we?" Pink smiled as she watched Jeezy walk out the door.

When Jeezy stepped foot in his house he saw Paige sitting on the couch fully dressed. "Hey baby you going somewhere?"

153

"No April said she was coming over in a minute and we supposed to be going shopping."

"I have to tell you something" Jeezy said taking a deep breath. He knew once he spilled the beans Paige was going to be heated. "April is not who you think she is."

"What do you mean" Paige said with a confused look on her face.

"First of all April's name isn't April. It's Pink and while you were locked up that's who I was getting money with."

Paige's eyes got watery. "Did you fuck her?"
Jeezy looked down at the floor before answering. "Yes."

Paige hopped up off the couch with the quickness and attacked Jeezy. She kicked and swung her arms wildly trying to rip Jeezy's eyes out. Jeezy quickly wrestled Paige down to the floor restraining her so she couldn't hit him no more. "Calm down baby."

"Fuck you Jeezy!" Paige yelled. "Let go of my arms" she said struggling to break free from his hold. "You got me walking around here looking stupid being best friends with some bitch you were fucking while I was locked up doing time for you!" she cried. "I lost three years of my life for you that I can't ever get back. Not to mention I almost got killed while I was in jail and you out here playing house with our next door neighbor!"

Just hearing that made Jeezy feel like shit. He knew he was dead wrong, but he called himself protecting Paige's feelings, but in all reality all he did was make things worse. "Baby I'm sorry."

"You're not sorry! So don't give me that sorry bullshit!" Paige yelled. "You were probably still fucking the bitch too weren't you!"

"No baby" Jeezy lied again as he got from off top of her. "Baby I'm sorry I wanted to tell you."

"But you didn't Jeezy" Paige cried. "I trusted you! I would've died for you! I would've done anything for you. All I asked in return was for you to keep it real with me and you couldn't even do that!"

"Baby believe me I wanted to tell you" Jeezy tried to explain. "I been broke things off with Pink way before you came home, but she threatened to kill you if I didn't continue to talk to her and I didn't want you to get hurt."

"You didn't want me to get hurt?" Paige echoed. "You need to be worried about that bitch cause she's the one that's about to get hurt" Paige said heading out the door.

"No baby just let it go" Jeezy said going after Paige. When Paige made it outside she saw Pink getting in her cocaine white Audi.

"Where do you think you are going bitch?" Paige yelled stepping on Pink's lawn. "Get out the car bitch!" "You said you was going to kill me well here I am" she said banging on the driver's window.
Pink smiled as she slowly backed out of her driveway.

"That's what I thought bitch!" Paige kicked the bumper on the Audi. Pink blew a kiss at Paige as she pulled away from the curb flying down the street.

"Come on baby let's go back in the house you making a scene" Jeezy said in a low voice.

"Fuck these neighbors!" Paige yelled as she stomped back inside the house.

"Baby I'm sorry I swear I..."

"I don't even want to hear it" Paige cut him off. "I have the biggest audition of my life tomorrow and I'd appreciate it if you didn't bother me for the rest of the night" Paige said.

Jeezy stood there with a stupid look on his face as he watched Paige storm up the stairs to their bedroom and slam the door behind her.

"I fucked up" Jeezy said to himself burying his head into his hands. He knew for sure once all this was over Paige would definitely leave him for good and he couldn't blame nobody but himself if she did.

***

Hov sat at his kitchen table with an assault rifle within arm's reach. He still couldn't believe him and his team managed to let the Gambino Brothers escape without a scratch on them. It really didn't matter because the Gambino Brothers were going to have to pay for what they did to Hov's son one way or another. Hov poured himself a shot of Vodka when he heard someone ringing his door bell. Hov looked through the peep hole and quickly opened the door. "Hey baby what's up?"

"I need to talk to you." Pink walked up in Hov's house crying.

"What's wrong baby" Hov asked his voice full of concern.

"I just got attacked" Pink cried. "My neighbor's boyfriend just attacked me" she lied. She knew Hov had a soft spot for her and hearing that she had been attacked would definitely grab his full attention.

"Calm down baby and start from the top" Hov said sitting Pink down on the couch.

"I was coming out of my house and out of nowhere my neighbor's boyfriend attacked me" Pink lied with a straight face.

"Don't worry about it baby I'mma take care of it" Hov said in a calm voice as he walked in the other room to take a phone call.

Pink had been seeing Hov for the past month and she still didn't know what he did for a living. Every time his phone rung Hov would always take the call in another room. Pink didn't know exactly what Hov did for a living, but from how secretive he was she figured it was something illegal. Minutes later Hov returned back to living room. "I have to go take care of something but I'll be back later" he said leaning down kissing Pink on the lips. "Don't leave until I get back" he told her as he made his exit.

Outside Alpo sat in the driver seat of his Range Rover waiting for Hov. Montana had wanted to see them and speak to them about what had went down the other night with the Gambino Brothers.

Never Be The Same

***

Montana sat in his office going over a few stock updates with his stock broker. Ever since the hit with the Gambino Brothers went sour he made sure he upped his security just to be on the safe side. Montana had money so he wasn't afraid of the Gambino Brothers. What bothered him was the fact that now he had to look over his shoulder every five minutes.

Montana quickly dismissed his stock broker when Hov and Alpo walked in his office. Once the stock broker was out of earshot Montana spoke. "How in the world did yall let the Gambino Brothers get away?"

"Them pussies' were running for their lives" Alpo replied. "I thought you said these guys were heartless killers? Those bitches ain't look like no killers to me."

"Trust me these guys are the real thing" Montana said. "And now since y'all missed the hit these wild cowboys are going to be on my ass."

"I still have my people's hunting for those clowns" Hov said in a calm tone. "They are going to have to pay for shooting my son."

"The easiest way to find those guys is to piss them off" Montana smiled. Then you wouldn't have to go looking for them, they would definitely come looking for you."

"You should have been told me that" Alpo said. He didn't like the Gambino Brothers or anybody else who thought they were bullet proof. His motto was simple, "you don't fuck with

158

me and I won't fuck with you", but now since his right hand man's son had been shot in an attempted robbery it was on.

"Listen I called you two down here cause I got some info for you" Montana said sliding a picture across the table to Hov. He looked at it for a few seconds. "Who is this bitch?"

"Her name is Peaches" Montana smiled. "One of my hoes, told me they heard her in the nail shop crying about how she had to leave her man Alex Gambino. Now if this is the same Alex Gambino I know then we got his ass. All yall have to do is follow the chick and wait for Alex to show up."

"You sure this is his bitch" Alpo asked while taking a look at the picture.

"Only one way to find out" Montana said. "I just hope y'all find them before they find me."

"I'm on it" Hov said as he and Alpo stood up to leave. "When I get a lead on this I'll give you a ring."

Montana replied with a simple head nod. He prayed that Hov and Alpo caught up with the Gambino Brothers before things got too out of hand.

***

Outside the Gambino Brothers pulled up across the street from Montana's house. Just as they were about to get out the car Alex spotted Hov and Alpo leaving.

"You see I told you Montana set us up" he pointed out. Victor grabbed his two 45's and was about to get out the car until Alex stopped him. "Hold up, one thing at a time. We are here for Montana. They're next."

Once the Range Rover was out of sight, the Gambino Brothers exited their car.

***

Montana sat in his hot tub, trying to relax and take his mind off of the Gambino Brothers. Just as he leaned his head back and rested his eyes they shot back open when the sound of loud gunfire could be heard coming from downstairs. Montana quickly hopped out the tub butt naked, dripping wet, slipping, and sliding all over the place.

Bits of broken glass crackled under Alex's boots as he made his way upstairs in search for Montana.

Upstairs Montana scrambled to the master bed room searching for a gun, but the footsteps he heard coming from behind him made him nervous to where he couldn't think straight.

"Looking for something" Alex asked cocking his shotgun. When Montana heard the paralyzing sound of the gun cock behind him he nearly shitted on himself. "Wait I can explain" he said turning around butt naked with his hands up in a surrendering position.

"It's not what you think."

"Oh really," Alex said with a smirk as he aimed his shotgun at Montana's leg and pulled the trigger. Montana hit the floor with a hard thud like he had been thrown off of a roof as he screamed out in pain clutching his leg.

"Please don't do this" Montana begged.

"Why did you set us up" Victor asked entering the bedroom.

"Because yall robbed a heavy hitter, a Made-guy," Montana said with pain written all over his face. "Someone that was untouchable."

"Everyone is touchable" Victor said putting another bullet in Montana's other leg. "Now who's the untouchable guy?"

"His name is Hov" Montana told him. "If you kill me the people I'm connected with will hunt you forever and they will find you."

"We look forward to it" Alex said blowing Montana's brains out to the other side of the room. Next on their list was Hov.

***

When Hov made it back home, he saw Pink sleeping on the couch. He smiled at how innocent she looked while she was asleep. Hov really liked Pink, but he needed to know a little bit more about her before he could take it to the next level with her. Hov and his crew were called "The Untouchables" no matter what crew went up against them Hov's crew always came out on top. Hov never had any problems. That's why when his son was shot it really messed with him. He couldn't believe someone had the balls to try and take something from him and shoot his innocent son in the process. Things like that didn't happen to made men. The beef between him and the Gambino Brothers wasn't business it was very personal.

"Hey baby I didn't even hear you come in" Pink yawned and stretched at the same time.

"You were looking so peaceful I didn't want to bother you" Hov said pouring himself a shot of dark liquor. Pink quickly went in the bathroom and brushed her teeth before she returned and gave Hov a big kiss. "I missed you while you were gone" she kissed him again.

"What's been on your mind? You have been kind of distant lately?"

"Just thinking about my son" Hov said honestly.

"So why don't you go get him and bring him here" Pink asked.

"Recently one of my other houses were robbed and in the process my son took a bullet to the leg. Now his mother is so scared that she took him and moved out of town" Hov said. "Now when I go to see him, he is so scared to be around me thinking someone is going to try to kill us."

All Pink could say was, "Damn". Just by looking at Hov she wouldn't have been able to tell that he was such a powerful player in the game. "Do you know who shot your son?"

"I have a possibility" Hov said not wanting to reveal too much information.

"I know just what you need" Pink said leading Hov upstairs to the master bedroom. Upstairs Pink stripped Hov naked and made him lay flat on his stomach. Then she slid on his back and gave him a nice massage. After the massage Pink rolled Hov onto his back and slid down on top of his already hard dick and rode him nice and slow.

I Need This Gig

Jeezy woke up on the couch when he heard movement in the kitchen. When he looked up he saw Paige in the kitchen dressed in a pair of black slacks and a nice black blouse standing in front of the counter making her something to eat.

"Good morning baby" Jeezy stretched.

"Hey" Paige replied dryly.

"Did you make me something to eat?"

"Why don't you tell your bitch to make you something to eat" Paige said still mad about the whole Pink situation. Jeezy knew better then to try and talk to her while she was in one of these kinds of moods so instead he just went upstairs to go take a shower.

When he returned back downstairs he noticed that Paige was gone. Jeezy pulled out his cell phone and sent her a text that said "Good luck on the audition today baby."

Jeezy sat on the couch and thought about everything he had been through in the last three years and asked himself was it worth it? Was it worth losing the best thing that had ever happened to him? No matter how many times he asked himself that question the answer was always the same; NO. Jeezy hated that he had to break the news to Paige the way he did, but he could no longer go another day being Pink's sex slave.

Jeezy's train of thought was broken when he heard a knock at his door. Thinking Paige must have forgot something, Jeezy opened the door without looking through the peephole. On the other side of the door stood Alpo and another man that stood nearly 7 feet tall.

"Can I help you" Jeezy asked.

"I'm looking for a Jeezy" Alpo said.

"I'm Jeezy" he answered. Once he said that, Alpo stole on Jeezy sending him stumbling back inside the house. Before Jeezy got a chance to catch his balance the 7 foot monster grabbed the back of his head and began raining knees into his stomach and chest area. Then he finished him off with a powerful uppercut.

"Stay the fuck away from Pink" Alpo huffed sending a sharp kick to Jeezy's ribs. "If I have to come back again, it ain't gone be no talking" Alpo said as he took a step back and hog spit in Jeezy's face. Alpo and the 7 foot man laughed loudly as they left Jeezy lying on the floor in the middle of his living room.

Jeezy stayed down for a few minutes trying to get his thoughts together before he peeled himself up off the floor and headed to the bathroom to see how bad the damage was. As he examined the big knot on his head, he desperately tried to figure out why the two men came to his house talking about stay away from Pink when it was him who wanted Pink to stay away from him.

Jeezy went to the kitchen and grabbed an ice pack from the freezer and placed it on the knot on his head as he went and grabbed his 40 caliber and sat in the living room hoping the two men came back again.

Lights, Camera, Action

Paige sat outside in the waiting area waiting for her number to be called so she could show the producers what she could do. She tried to read over her lines one last time, but she wasn't in the right frame of mind. Every time she closed her eyes she would see pictures of Jeezy and Pink having wild sex. Paige still couldn't believe that Jeezy let her become best friends with the chick that he was fucking while she was locked up without telling her. All of the trust that she had for Jeezy flew out the window after a stunt like that. Not only did Jeezy cheat on her, but he made her look stupid in the process and that's the part that hurt Paige the most.

"I can't do this" Paige said to herself. Just as she was about to get up to leave a white lady holding a clipboard called her name.

Paige took a deep breath, put on her professional face, and entered the audition room.

"How are you doing my name is Mike" the producer said extending his hand.
"Nice to meet you Mike, I'm Paige" she said as the two shook hands.

"You'll be reading from pages fifty-five to sixty. Good luck" Mike said taking a seat with the rest of his staff.

Paige relaxed herself as she read her lines. It just so happened that the scene was a dramatic one so it was easy for

Paige to shed a few tears to give a more dramatic performance. Especially with all the drama that was going on in her life right now.

When Paige finished her performance Mike and his staff gave her a standing ovation.

"That was great!" Mike smiled. "Do me a favor and wait outside for a few minutes. I would like to have a word with you when this is all over."

Paige could tell by the glow on his face that she had gotten the part hands down. "Okay I'll be right out front."

When Paige made it back to the waiting area she said a quick prayer thanking God for giving her another opportunity to do what she loved to do. Paige was so excited she pulled out her cell phone and was about to call Jeezy and tell him the good news, but after thinking about it she slid her iPhone back inside her purse.

She hated having to be like this with Jeezy, but what he did crossed the line in her eyes. If he had to sleep with someone else the least he could of did was keep the chick away from her and not allow the chick to move right next door. The more Paige thought about it the angrier she became and the more she started making up her own version of Pink's and Jeezy's relationship.

Paige decided to pull out her ear phones and listen to some music hoping it would take her mind off of Jeezy. Just as Paige got ready to stick her ear phones in her iPhone she looked up and saw Pink heading in her direction. At first she thought she was seeing things. The harder she looked the more certain she was that it really was Pink.

"Remain calm" Paige told herself while taking a deep breath. When she saw the jeans and Ugg boots and head scarf that Pink was wearing she already knew what time it was. Just as Paige stood to her feet Pink rushed her swinging wildly. The two collided like two rams. As both women tried to kill the other one, Pink and Paige crashed through the little coffee table in the waiting area as they both scrapped like their lives depended on it.

Mike and his staff rushed out of the audition room and tried to separate the two women.

"Bitch, stay the fuck away from my man," Pink yelled. "If I catch you next to my man again I'mma beat your ass again!"

"You wish that was your man bitch." "You weren't anything but something to do to pass the time" Paige yelled as security escorted Pink out of the building.

Once Pink was gone Paige realized she had just acted like an animal. She had the same feeling that she had when she was locked up. She looked over at Mike and when he rolled his eyes at her and went back inside the audition room, right then and there she knew she had just fucked up her second chance of being an actor.

"Ma'am I'm going to have to ask you to leave the building" Security said sternly. Paige exited the building with her head hung low. Her confidence and self-esteem was at an all-time low. She hopped in her car and headed straight to the liquor store to get her self something to sip on.

***

Jeezy sat on the couch listening to The Blue Print 3, thinking about how he could make things back right with Paige. He knew he had messed up big time, but was willing to do anything to get back on her good side.

Jeezy's head snapped to the right when he heard someone coming through the front door. When he saw Paige walk through the front door with her hair all wild and a few scratches on her face Jeezy quickly rushed to her side. "Baby what happened? Are you alright?"

"I'm fine" Paige said pushing Jeezy away from her.

"What happened?"

"Your bitch came down to my audition and ruined any chance of me getting back into the acting world" Paige said looking Jeezy up and down. "This is all your fault!" "I hate you," she said as tears rolled down her face as she headed upstairs and slammed the door.

"Fuck!" Jeezy cursed loudly as he turned and punched a hole in the wall. He could no longer take all of Pink's games. It was time to end it all once and for all. Pink had ruined him, his woman, his happiness, and now his woman's job. It was now time for her to pay.

Jeezy stormed out of the house, hopped in his Benz, and headed towards the strip club.

I Want You Back

Alex stood in the bar area of his house having a drink with his brother. He was trying to figure out the best way to tell his brother that he had made a mistake by getting back in the game and that he missed Peaches. With what he already had saved away plus what he and Victor got from Montana's safe, Alex never had to work another day of his life.

"What you over there thinking about bro," Victor asked pouring both of them another drink.

"I miss Peaches" Alex admitted.

"Not that bitch again," Victor huffed. "What is it with you and that chick?"

"I just realized that this shit we doing isn't worth it anymore," Alex said. "We're rich now. It's time for us to enjoy the fruits of our labor."

"What about Hov," Victor asked. "We're just going to let him off the hook?"

"It's not worth it" Alex said simply. "We almost got our heads blown off the other night for what; for money that we don't even need."

"I know what your problem is" Victor shook his head in disgust. "You're letting this money change you. You're turning into one of them high class rich cock suckers!"

Alex knew his younger brother would have a problem with his decision, but he didn't care. His mind was already made up. Peaches was worth more to him than a couple of measly dollars and if his brother didn't like it then so be it. "You need to open your eyes and smell the roses before it's too late."

"Fuck you!" Victor sat his drink down like he was ready to get busy. "You walk out that door this time and you are no longer my brother!"

Alex finished up the last of his drink before he replied. "I love you and you'll always be my brother no matter what," he said as he made his exit.

His life felt incomplete without Peaches in it and he could no longer torture himself. He needed his baby back.

***

Jeezy pulled up in front of the strip club and hopped out of his Benz and left the engine running. When Jeezy stepped foot in the club he headed straight to the bar and ordered himself a strong drink. He scanned the club to see if he saw Pink anywhere around.

After a forty-five minute wait Jeezy finally spotted Pink over in the corner giving some john a lap dance. He downed the rest of his drink in one gulp before heading over in her direction.

The closer Jeezy got to Pink, the angrier he became. He couldn't believe he had let a chick come in his life and turn it upside down and for that Pink was going to have to pay.

When he got within arm's reach of Pink he tapped her on the shoulder. When Pink turned around and saw Jeezy standing there she smiled as if she was happy to see him.

"Heeeey baby" she said as if the two were the best of friends. Pink leaned in for a hug and Jeezy smacked the shit out of her. Pink's head violently jerked back from the impact as she spun around and to the floor.

When Pink's body hit the floor Jeezy stood over her and rained down punches on Pink's exposed face. It took several johns to finally get him off of her.

"Bitch, stay the fuck away from my family," Jeezy screamed as two big bouncers now escorted him out the club and tossed him out into the street.

Jeezy quickly got up off the ground and jogged back to his Benz and headed back home.

On the ride home Jeezy thought about what he had just done. It may not have been the right thing to do, but it was damn sure necessary.

When Jeezy pulled into his driveway, he looked up and saw that the bedroom light was still on which meant that Paige was still up. He made his way in the house and headed straight for the bedroom. "Baby we need to talk" he said busting in the room.
"No" Paige said flatly. "I don't feel like talking to you. Don't you think you've ruined my life enough already?"

"Look baby I'm sorry about everything that happened while you were locked up, but all I was trying to do was get money while you were away so when you came home you could be comfortable" he explained. "How was I supposed to know that this psycho chick was going to fall in love with me and start acting crazy?"

"If the tables were reversed and you just got out of jail and the nigga who I was fucking lived right next door and the two of you became best friends, how would that make you feel?" "EXACTLY" she said not even giving him a chance to answer. "You men are all the same. Yall can dish it out but you damn sure can't take it!"

"Baby I know how you feel. Just know that my intentions were good" Jeezy said. "No matter what, I'm going to love you."

"You don't love me, you love Pink" Paige said out of jealously. She knew that Jeezy would never do anything to intentionally hurt her, but at the moment her feelings were hurt and she didn't want to just take him back so easily. "Did you check on your girlfriend today?"

"Yeah I just came from her job" Jeezy told her.

"Oh so after all this you still messing around with the bitch," Paige said ready to act a fool.

"I went to her job and beat her ass baby!" Jeezy shook his head. "I don't play when it comes to you and you know that." "Well that ain't going to stop me from beating her ass again the next time I see her " Paige said still upset that Pink had messed up her wonderful audition. Not to mention she had embarrassed and humiliated her in front of everyone.

"If moving will make you feel better, then we can. I don't care what it's going to take to get you back. As long as I can have you I'll do it."

"Just give me a day or two to think and then I'll let you know what's what, but right now I just want to be alone."

"Yes baby" Jeezy said obeying Paige's wishes. "I'll be on the couch if you need me" he said making his exit.

Love in the Air

Alex pulled up in front of Peaches mother's house and killed the engine. After being away from Peaches for two weeks he realized that he needed her in his life more than he thought he did. No matter what was going on she always made him feel special, like he was too good to be robbing people. She had a way of just making him feel worth way more than he was and he loved her for that.

Alex stepped out his truck, walked up to the front door and rang the doorbell.

***

A block away Alpo sat in a low key Honda watching Alex's every move. Montana was right about Peaches. She definitely led Alex straight to them. Alpo and his 7 foot friend watched as Alex entered Peaches mother's house.

"We going to tighten his ass up as soon as he comes out that bitch," Alpo said cocking the back slide on his Mac-11. The 7 foot monster replied by simply cocking back his automatic weapon.

***

"How are you doing Ms. Jackson" Alex said politely. "Is Peaches home?"

"Yes, sure Alex come right on in" Ms. Jackson said giving Alex a bear hug. "Yeah she's right upstairs in her room."

"Okay thanks" Alex said quickly heading upstairs to Peaches room. Alex entered Peaches room without even knocking on the door. "Hey"

"Oh hey" Peaches said turning around in shock. "Hey Alex what are you doing here?"

"I came to see you" Alex replied. "I need you back in my life."

Peaches looked at him for a second. "I don't think so"

"What do you mean you don't think so" Alex echoed?

"You heard me" Peaches said raising her tone a bit. "I don't have time to play these games with you. One minute you love me and the next minute you love the streets. Like come on make up your mind."

"Baby I'm sorry" Alex apologized. "I finally see what you were saying about this street shit. I just never had anybody to love me before until I met you and I refuse to lose you."

"Sounds good" Peaches rolled her eyes. She was still upset by the way he had chosen to go run the streets and then be with her.

"How do I know if I take you back you won't just do the same thing again?"

"Baby I give you my word," Alex said. "I can't and won't live without you."

"Well I got a date tonight so I don't know what to tell you," Peaches said coldly.

"Damn you got a new man already?" Alex face crumbled up.

"Nigga I haven't heard not one word from you in two weeks" Peaches said. "And then you just pop up at my mom's house out the blue, talking about you want me back. I don't know what you think this is, but you are not going to just be playing games with my heart whenever you feel like it!"

"Baby nobody is playing games."

"Well that's what it seems like to me" Peaches countered. She didn't have time to play games with Alex. He didn't know what he wanted so it was time for her to move on. "Anyway, like I said I have a date tonight" she said in a nasty tone.

"Why are you acting like this towards me" Alex asked. "I know you love me, so why are you pretending not to?"

"Because" Peaches began, "I gave you my all and that still wasn't good enough to keep you, so I don't know what to do."

"Give me another chance; please" Alex asked.

"Give me a few days to think about it because what you did to me really hurt me" Peaches said.

"Well you need to cancel your date."

"No" Peaches replied. "You don't just pop up out the blue at my mom's house because you decide you want me back and tell me to cancel my date! Sorry, but it doesn't work like that!"

Their conversation was interrupted when Ms. Jackson lightly knocked on the door. "Peaches you got somebody downstairs at the door waiting for you" she announced.

"Oh so that's your new boyfriend downstairs," Alex asked with his voice full of jealousy.

"None of your business" Peaches replied as she headed downstairs. When she reached the bottom step she heard Alex's footsteps coming right behind hers.

"Hey we are in my mother's house. Don't start any shit" she warned.

"I'm not. I just want to talk to the guy" Alex lied. He couldn't believe that Peaches already had someone new that fast. He knew how he ended things with her was wrong, but he was back to make things right. He wasn't about to let some new guy stand in his way.

Peaches opened the front door and on the other side stood a man with dreads, gold teeth, in his mid-twenties, and with his pants sagging off his ass.

"What's up baby are you ready roll?" Gold teeth smiled.
"She ain't rolling anywhere" Alex said stepping outside not wanting to disrespect Ms. Jackson's house.

"Who's this chump" Gold teeth asked looking over at Peaches.

"Nobody" Peaches said quickly. "He was just leaving."

Just as Gold Teeth got ready to say another word Alex pulled out his P89 and whacked him across the face with it. Alex stood over the man as he pistol whipped the man until he lost feeling in his hands.

"What is wrong with you" Peaches screamed looking at Alex like he was a monster. Seconds later Ms. Jackson came outside to see what all the commotion was about.

"I'm sorry" Alex apologized. He was about to say something else until he saw a quick blur moving from the corner of his eye.

Before he could tell Peaches to get down, he watched as three bullets to the chest spun her body around like a merry go round.

When Alex looked up, he saw two men with big guns moving in on him. He quickly sent two shot in their direction as he took off on foot down the street. Alex put his head down and ran at a full sprint trying to avoid the two gunmen. He fired two reckless shots over his shoulder as he quickly dashed behind a parked car to gather his thoughts.

Alpo shot out all the windows on the car that Alex stood behind trying to shake him up. Alpo signaled to his 7 foot partner to take one side while he took the other.

Alex took a deep breath as shattered glass rained down on the top of his head. With no other choice on the count of three Alex popped up from behind the parked car firing away. Four of his bullets found a home in the tall man's chest, but as the tall man went down he got off a single shot that pierced though

Alex's thigh causing him to drop down to one knee. "Shit!" he cursed as pain shot through his entire body.

When Alpo saw his partner go down he immediately opened fire on the parked car as he moved in for the kill. Alex quickly popped up from behind the car again and before he could get a shot off, two shots to the chest had dropped him. His head bounced off the concrete like a basketball, as his gun flew out of his hand.

Once Alpo saw Alex's body hit the ground he smiled as he took off running back to the Honda. With all the dead bodies lying around he wasn't trying to stick around to see what happened. He hopped in his Honda and burnt rubber.

Can't Let It Go

Paige sat in the hot tub trying to get her mind off of all the things that had been going on in her life, but it seemed liked the more she tried not to think about it, the more she would think about it.

Jeezy had been doing everything in his power to make Paige feel comfortable, but Paige just couldn't find it in her heart to forgive him. Of course she still had love for him, but now every time she thought about Jeezy, Pink would somehow end up in her thoughts and ruin any chance of her forgiving Jeezy.

As Paige sat in the tub she thought about how Pink had really tried to end her acting career. A beat down wasn't going to be enough. Paige wanted Pink to hurt the way she was hurting.

Paige hopped out the tub, dried off, threw on a navy blue sweat suit, and headed straight for the closet. Inside she grabbed her baseball bat that she kept in there for protection and headed downstairs.

When Jeezy saw Paige coming downstairs carrying a baseball bat he immediately hopped up off the couch. "Baby, what are you doing with that bat," he asked.

Paige ignored him passing by Jeezy like he was invisible as she headed outside. Jeezy sighed loudly as he followed Paige outside to see what she had in mind.

Outside Paige gripped her bat in a tight two handed grip and she swung the bat into the front window of Pink's house. All Jeezy could do was shake his head as he watched the glass window shatter into little pieces. She then winded the bat up again, and took out another window, followed by another window, followed by another window, until all of the windows in the front of Pink's house were busted out.

"Bitch you are fucking with the wrong one" she said as if Pink could hear her. Jeezy looked at all the busted out windows and felt bad for even putting Paige in a situation like this. He had gotten them into this mess and it was he who was going to get them out.

I Don't Play That

Hov sat in the living room watching the Giants and Eagles game when Alpo entered his house with a smile on his face.

"I hope you got some good news for me" Hov said not bothering to look up from the TV.

"One of the Gambino Brothers is now officially gone" Alpo bragged.

"Say word!"

"Word to my mother!" "I shot that nigga up outta his shoes," Alpo boasted, "him and his bitch!"

Hov smiled, "one down and one more to go!"

Hov and Alpo's conversation was interrupted when Pink entered the house with her face looking a bloody mess.

"What happened to you baby," Hov asked shooting to his feet.

"Jeezy," she cried. "He came down to my job and attacked me."

Hov quickly turned and faced Alpo. "I thought I asked you rough that clown up?"

"I did" Alpo replied. "He must have caught her afterwards."

"You alright baby," Hov asked sitting her down gently on the couch.

Pink played to be more hurt then she really was. She knew Hov would go crazy if she came home all beat up.

"You want me to run down on that clown and clap him," Alpo asked.

"Nah I want you to go over there and bring him to me," Hov ordered. "I wanna do this clown myself!"

"Not a problem!" Alpo smiled as he got up and left.

"Don't worry about nothing baby. I'mma handle that Nigga for you."

Pink wanted to smile so badly. Everything was going just as she planned it. Hov was going to get Jeezy out of the picture and then she'd be able to get rid of Paige once and for all.

"What's up with you and this nigga," Hov asked. "You used to fuck around with him or something?"

"I went out to eat with him once and then out the blue he started acting funny" Pink lied. "I think he had a girl and was trying to have his cake and eat it too. His girlfriend must have found out and then that's when he started bugging out."

"I'll take care of it" Hov said already thinking about what he was going to do to Jeezy when he got him in his sight.

Back From the Dead

Alex eyes shot open as he nervously looked around trying to figure out where he was. He winced in pain as he sat up realizing that he was naked. "Where the fuck am I," he said to himself as he looked over to the right and saw his bullet proof vest sitting on a chair with two holes around the chest area. His body felt like he had been hit by a car and he couldn't remember anything that had happened. Alex looked over to his right and saw his P89 sitting on top of the nightstand.

Just as Alex tried to get out of the bed he heard someone turn the knob and enter the room. He quickly reached over and grabbed his P89 and aimed it at the person standing in the door way.

"Put that gun down. I'm not here to hurt you," the woman said sitting a plate of food down on the bed.

"Who are you and where are my clothes," Alex asked with his gun still aimed at the woman.

"My name is Elizabeth and your clothes are in the dryer. They needed to be washed" she said. "Here eat up."

Alex slowly put his P89 down and grabbed a piece of fried chicken from off the plate and took a bite. "How did I get here?"

"I was sitting in my living room watching TV when I heard a million shots being fired right outside my door" Elizabeth said." Once the gunfire ended I peeked out my blinds and saw you lying on my lawn. I went outside and saw that you still had a pulse so I dragged you in the house before the cops arrived."

"Thank you" Alex said shoveling a spoon full of rice into his mouth. "Why did you help me?"

"Hispanic man, having a shootout in the middle of the street," Elizabeth smiled. "I just figured I would do a good deed and keep you out of jail."

"I appreciate it."

"By the way you owe me a new car. That was my car you took cover behind" Elizabeth informed him.

Alex smirked. "I'll take care of it for you."

"Okay well your body needs to rest for at least two days, so make yourself at home. If you need anything just let me know" Elizabeth said exiting the room giving Alex his privacy.

Alex finished off his food, laid back down, and shut his eyes. His body was still sore and needed rest.

Rise and Shine

After all the shit Paige talked she winded up forgiving Jeezy and took him back but only if he promised that within a month's time they would have a new house somewhere far away from Pink and all of her drama.

Jeezy had come clean and told Paige everything that happened while she was locked up. He even told her about the rich African man that he and Pink had murdered together.

After listening to the full story Paige came to the conclusion that Pink was really crazy and she had mental problems. As she lay asleep with her head resting on Jeezy's chest, she heard a noise coming from downstairs. Paige tried to ignore the noise, but seconds later she heard another noise that sounded like someone downstairs was digging in her kitchen drawers and cabinets. "Baby wake up" she shook Jeezy awaking him from a deep sleep.

"What's up baby," Jeezy asked not even bothering to open his eyes.

"Somebody is downstairs in our house baby" Paige said in a strong whisper. Jeezy opened his eyes and listened carefully.

"You heard that" Paige asked excitedly as she heard the noise again. "Go downstairs and check it out."

Never Be The Same

Jeezy slid out of bed and grabbed his 40 caliber off the nightstand as he headed downstairs to see what the noise was. As he reached the top of the steps he saw three men wearing ski-mask creeping up the stairs.

"Fuck outta here" Jeezy said to himself as he opened fire on the three gunmen sending them crashing back down the stairs.

Paige's body jumped out of fear when she heard the loud thunderous shots echo throughout the quiet house.

Jeezy slowly made his way downstairs to see if anyone else was in his house. He eased his way through the dark living room.

"Hey fam," a voice called out. When Jeezy turned around a baseball bat collided with the side of his head knocking him out cold.

"Somebody come and drag this mufucka up outta here," Alpo said standing over Jeezy's unconscious body. His orders were to bring Jeezy back alive.

"Hey I'm calling the police" Paige said at the top of the steps holding her cell phone to her ear.

"Snitching ass bitch" Alpo said as he tossed the bat at Paige as he and his crew left with Jeezy's body. The bat landed three feet away from Paige as she gave the 911 operator her address.

Twenty minutes later Paige's home was filled with police officers. She answered all of their questions the best way she could without giving up too much information and/or incriminating herself in the process.

It's On

Victor sat in Alex's crib loading up the M-16 that sat before him. It had been five days since he had heard from Alex. He had been watching the news so when he heard that Peaches and her mother had been gunned down he figured the killers must have gunned down Alex as well. The cops just hadn't found his body yet. Victor didn't know for sure who was responsible for his brother's murder, but all signs pointed to Hov.

Honestly Victor didn't care who had killed his brother the entire city was going to have to pay starting with Hov and his crew. Victor strapped on his bullet proof vest and grabbed his M-16 and went out the door.

***

Alex woke up and slid out of the bed. His body was still a little sore, but he had rested long enough. He stepped out the room still butt naked and entered the living room looking for Elizabeth.

Alex stopped dead in his tracks when he saw Elizabeth sitting at the kitchen table cleaning a machine gun. He quietly stood and watched as Elizabeth broke down the machine gun, cleaned it, and put it back together in less than a minute.

"Where did you learn how to do that" Alex asked startling Elizabeth.

"Oh" Elizabeth said quickly putting the big gun away. "I didn't even hear you get up."

"What kind of shit are you into" Alex asked suspiciously.

"Tell me what you do for a living and I'll tell you what I do for a living; deal?" Elizabeth extended her hand.

"Deal" Alex shook her hand. "Me and my brother go around robbing anything that ain't nailed down to the floor" Alex told her.

"You wouldn't happen to be one of "The Gambino Brothers" would you" Elizabeth smiled.

"That's me Alex Gambino," he said proudly.

"Impressive" Elizabeth said. "I've heard about you and your brother's work, but if you ask my opinion I think y'all are in the wrong profession."

"What line of work are you into" Alex asked.

"Banks" Elizabeth said with an evil smirk on her face.

Alex laughed out loud. "So you mean to tell me you rob banks?"

Elizabeth didn't reply instead she tossed a month old newspaper at Alex's chest. Alex caught the paper and looked at the headline on the front page that read: "FIVE DEAD IN A SUCCESSFUL BANK ROBBERY"

"So" Alex began. "I know you don't take down these banks alone."

"No, I have another partner" she said looking down at Alex's package. "We could use two more good men if you're interested."

"I don't know about banks" Alex said. "Plus I was thinking..."

Elizabeth silenced Alex by pressing her full lips against his as she worked him into to stiffness with her hands. She couldn't resist all that temptation that stood in front of her any longer. She had to have it. She forced Alex back inside the room and shut the door behind her.

If I Die Today

When Jeezy finally came back around, he saw a bunch of thugs standing around him in a small room. He didn't know what was going on, but the one thing he did know was that today was the day that he was going to die. "Where am I?"

"Shut the fuck up!" Alpo huffed as he smacked the shit out of Jeezy. "Didn't I tell you what was going to happen if I had to come back?"

"What's this all about" Jeezy asked confused.

"I told you to stay the fuck away from Pink" Alpo snarled as he got ready to slap Jeezy again until Hov stepped in and stopped him.

"What's your obsession with Pink" Hov asked. "Why can't you stay away from her?"

"What are you talking about" Jeezy asked. With the quickness of a cat Hov turned and snuffed Jeezy.

"I'm giving you a chance to tell your side of the story before you die," Hov told him.

"No you got it all wrong" Jeezy said spitting out blood. "That bitch Pink is crazy. I was dealing with her while my girl was locked up and when I tried to break it off with her she went crazy."

"She started stalking me and she even attacked my girl!"

"Bullshit" Hov spat.

"That's my word" Jeezy told him. "The bitch had me doing sexual favors for her so she wouldn't tell my girl."

"This nigga is lying his ass off" Alpo cut in. He just wanted to hurt somebody.

"When was the last time you smashed" Hov asked curiously?

"Umm" Jeezy said checking his memory. "About a week ago."

Those words cut Hov like a knife. He was really starting to like Pink and for some strange reason he believed Jeezy. Hov pulled out his phone and dialed Pink's number but it went straight to voice mail.

"Do you know where Pink is now" Hov asked.

"If I know her like I think I do, then she just went home and saw all her windows busted out and she's headed to my house" Jeezy told him. "We have to get over there quick before she kills my fiancé!"

Hov thought about it for a second before he cut Jeezy loose. "I'm going with you" Hov said. "He wanted to see for himself if Pink was as crazy as Jeezy made her out to be and if Jeezy was lying he was going to kill him.

Only the Strong Survive

Paige stood in the kitchen cooking dinner. She had to do something to stop worrying about Jeezy and if he was safe. She had been praying all day and inside she felt that wherever Jeezy was the Lord was going to bring him back to her in one piece like he always did.

If and when Jeezy made it back in one piece the first thing Paige planned on doing was moving to another city and starting over fresh from scratch. She didn't care if she had to work a regular job as long as she and Jeezy were together she didn't care.

As Paige stood at the counter cutting up a piece of raw steak, she looked up at the front door when she heard keys jingling at the door. Paige's face lit up. She just knew her prayers had been answered. Her smile quickly turned upside down when she saw Pink come through the front door holding a hunting knife in her hand.

"How the fuck did you get the keys to my house" Paige asked.

"Bitch that's the last thing you need to be worrying about" Pink said coldly as she locked the door behind her. When Paige looked down at the hunting knife that Pink carried, she already knew what time it was. She grabbed a butcher's knife from out of the drawer and exited the kitchen.

Paige told herself once she was released from prison that she would leave that jail shit back in jail, but this was a different story right now. It was either kill or be killed.

"I'm sorry it had to come down to this, but my mother always told me when you come across something you love, you better be ready to die for it" Pink said.

"Jeezy is my fiancé" Paige said dragging out the word fiancé. "I'll die for my man because I know he'll do the same for me! Would he die for you bitch?"

That's all it took to set it off. Pink lunged towards Paige and took a swipe at her. Paige jumped back out of her reach as the two circled each other talking shit. Paige took a step forward taking a swipe at Pink's face. Pink leaned back and weaved the knife in the air and sliced Paige across her stomach reopening the scar she got while she was in jail.

Paige grabbed her stomach and took a step back.

"Come on you scary ass bitch" Pink taunted as she lunged forward again. This time Paige caught her wrist and sliced Pink across her face causing her to drop the hunting knife. Pink touched her face and when her hand came away bloody she let out a loud scream. It sounded like an animal had been wounded instead of a woman screaming.

"Put that knife down and let's handle this shit woman to woman" Pink said putting up her hands.

Paige smirked as she saw the blood leaking from Pink's face. "You're not even worth it" she said tossing her knife down to the floor.

Once the knife hit the floor Pink charged at Paige rushing her back into the wall unit that rested in the living room. Paige's head bounced off the entertainment system knocking her out cold. Pink quickly hopped up on her feet and began stomping Paige as if she was trying to stomp her through the floor.

"Stupid ass bitch!" Pink huffed kicking Paige in her face one last time. She caught her breath before walking back over to where her hunting knife rested. "Bitch I told you Jeezy was my man" Pink said as she plunged the hunting knife through Paige's heart. "Die bitch!" she yelled as she repeatedly stabbed Paige's lifeless body until her arms got tired and she didn't have the energy to stab her anymore.

Pink stood to her feet and smiled. Finally she had gotten rid of Paige. Now her and Jeezy could finally live happily ever after and be a family, so she thought.

Pink snapped out of her trance when she heard the front door open and saw Jeezy, Hov, Alpo, and two other soldiers walk through the front door.

When Jeezy saw Paige laid out on the floor covered in blood, his legs got weak. He rushed over to her. "No! No! No!" he cried melting down to his knees.

Hov looked on in shock. He couldn't believe what he was seeing. This was a side of Pink he had never seen before.

Jeezy cried over Paige's body as all of the memories the two shared flashed before his eyes. Paige's cold lifeless eyes stared up at him. Jeezy closed Paige's eyes and kissed her on the forehead as he removed the hunting knife that was sticking out of her chest. He gripped it tightly as he slowly rose to his feet.

"I did this for us daddy" Pink said with a proud look on her face.

"Now we can finally be a family" she smiled. "No more distractions! No more nothing, just me and you like old times" she smiled. "We can get married and move somewhere where it's hot."

As Jeezy walked up to Pink, he felt sorry for her because she really had a mental problem and needed serious help.

"Can I have a hug baby" Pink asked with open arms. Jeezy leaned and hugged Pink tightly.

"I love you daddy" Pink whispered in Jeezy's ear.

"I love you too" Jeezy said as he plunged the hunting knife in Pink's stomach and twisted the handle. A tear escaped Jeezy's eye as he hugged Pink tightly until her body finally collapsed in his arms.

Deep down in Jeezy's heart he still had love for Pink. He didn't want to have to kill her but at the end of the day he was left with no choice.

"You a'ight," Hov asked from the sideline. Jeezy gently laid Pink's body down and replied with a simple head nod.

"We gotta get up outta here before the cops come" Hov said.

"Don't worry about any money. I'll give you a job working for me."

"Nah yall go ahead. I'm going to stay here," Jeezy said as tears streamed down his face. "Without Paige I don't have a life and I might as well rot in jail" he said in a defeated tone.

"Don't even talk like that" Hov said as he gave his goons a signal for them to go get Jeezy up out of the house by any means necessary. "I'm not just going to sit here and leave you like that especially since..." Hov's words got caught in his throat when he saw the front door bust open and Victor step inside holding a M-16.

"What up" Victor said as he squeezed the trigger and waved his arms back and forth until everyone in the house was dead. "That's for my brother" he said out loud as he back peddled out the door and hopped back in his car.

As Victor drove back to Alex's house he wondered what his next move was going to be. He felt alone in the world without Alex. Ever since he was a kid Alex had always come up with all the bright ideas, but now with Alex gone Victor had no idea what his next move was going to be.

The only thing he knew now was that he was going to have to come up with something sooner than later. When Victor stepped foot back in the house he almost shitted on himself when he saw Alex and some chick sitting at the bar area having a drink.

"About time you got back. I was about to start getting worried," Alex smiled.

"When and where," Victor said at a loss for words. He didn't know what to say. He was just happy that his brother was alive. "I thought you were dead" he said hugging Alex tightly. He didn't want to let him go.

"Come on you know it's going to take more than some amateurs to take me out" Alex countered.

Victor looked over at the chick sitting next to Alex. "Who's the chick?"

"I want to introduce you to the newest member of The Gambino Family" Alex said. "This here is Elizabeth and she's going to help us take our bank accounts to another level. No more robbing drug dealers. It's time to step our game up."

"Okay well spit it out mufucka! What we going to be doing now" Victor asked curiously.

"What you know about banks" Elizabeth asked with a smirk.

TO BE CONTINUED!!!!

Never Be The Same

Now Available On Paperback

SILK WHITE

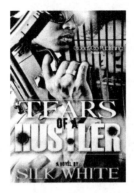

Good2GoFilms Present:

BLACK BARBIE THE MOVIE STARRING SILK WHITE

ORDER NOW FROM

WWW.GOOD2GOFILMS.COM

$7.99

NO WAY OUT THE MOVIE

STARRING SILK WHITE

Never Be The Same

www.silkwhite.com

www.good2gopublishing.com

www.good2gofilms.com

CPSIA information can be obtained at www.ICGtesting.com
Printed in the USA
LVOW04s1835020915

452548LV00018B/863/P

9 780615 630175